Marcienne Martin

I0654892

# *Words*
# *and Fiction*

Editions Dedicaces

WORDS AND FICTION

[Mots et fictions, translated from French by Caroline Andreea Zgortea]

Copyright © 2015 by Editions Dedicaces LLC

Published by:
    Editions Dedicaces LLC
    12759 NE Whitaker Way, Suite D833
    Portland, Oregon, 97230
    www.dedicaces.us

**Library of Congress Cataloging-in-Publication Data**
    Martin, Marcienne
        Words and Fiction, by Marcienne Martin.
        p. cm.
        ISBN-13: 978-1-77076-518-4 (alk. paper)
        ISBN-10: 1-77076-518-2 (alk. paper)

Marcienne Martin

# *Words and Fiction*

*The universe (that others call the library) is made of an
Indefinite number, and perhaps infinite, of hexagonal galleries, with
vast air shafts bordered by low railings in the
center.
Of each of these hexagons we can see the lower
and superior floors, interminably.
The distribution of the galleries is invariable.*

*My solitude takes comfort in this elegant hope.*

*Library of Babel
JORGE LOUIS BORGES
Fictions, Gallimard, Paris, 1983, p. 71.*

*To CORINNE BELLAY-MACHTOU*

*To ALAIN BELLAY*

# Table of Contents

# Voyage to the country of Anthuriums

Ruddy and swollen banisters in the center, trees playing the green declination on female watermarks, the Tahitian window opens to the soul of my unknown companion: Matisse. For this painter, I have become an obsession. May be because of my skin that the milky color disdained in favor of tones more in harmony with the land of Africa, which is also that of the golden almond. My hair is split into thousands of tiny loops that gather heat and sunlight without shame, as to the color of my iris, it is reminiscent of coffee beans wrapped in a pretty piece silk cambric that this painter had sent me. I look at myself and the image of an unknown man passes between my reflection and the mirror. The letters he sends me are delivered by special messenger and accompanied, sometimes by a flower of the islands: the Anthurium is also called "tongues of fire" in my epistolary. I wait every day the written murmurs of the great painter. I read his last letter in which he invites me "to a journey punctuated by a trembling heart".

Strange encounter, the one I made with Matisse. A friend of mine had invited me to an exhibition of his works. She had told me about distant and wild islands, unknown flowers and vibrant colors: I was seduced. I found there very dear friends and also, light relationships and I was waiting impatiently to meet the artist. He didn't show. Only an elderly man bent over my hand, which he barely touched, "Henri at your... service", then he left. I returned very late, tired and bored of this vain expectation. The next day, I received a bunch of flowers: lily crush, orchids and amaryllis, ranged in all ranges of red.

The boat has just left. Matisse wrote that he would wait for me at Papeete. In the cabin he reserved for me, three Anthuriums are placed on the shelf next to my bunk. In the shadow of their corollas, three large iridescent pearls are aligned: white, black and pink. A small card accompanies these gifts; it appears to have been sent from Polynesia: "My dearest with the skin the color of burnt almonds, may these beads adorn your lovely throat and my fiery tongues caress your body!"

Leaning against the railing, I noticed an elderly man whose glance seemed to draw me. I seem to recognize this gentleman Henri, met at the exhibition. Is Matisse like this man? I have to join him at the Stuart Hotel, where he wrote, he would wait for me and make me discover these islands at the end of the world. The wind blows and the sea sprays wet the folds of my silk green dress, which are pressed against my legs. They are drawn as a billhook. Henri is absorbed by the spectacle. The next day, the captain gives me a sort of painting: a feminine body carved in a blue lagoon paper and pasted on rigid and pearled cardboard. I seem to recognize my legs, drawn by the water.

Letters and gifts from Matisse arrive randomly in my cabin. There was one week, in the middle of the journey, where nothing happened. Neither frivolous card or flower. These eight days seemed very long. I opened my leather trunk and I got out, one by one, the dresses I had brought. The one that was my favorite, was the color of straw with tonal stripes. I walked on the deck and the men looked at me. Sometimes, I regretted having accepted this journey without knowing who was actually waiting for me on the Tahitian island. Eight days of boredom, of stretches of sea and dazzling sun. On the ninth day, I found a Gardenia flower attached to a pin filled with diamond chips. Then, I closed my eyes and thought of my future encounter with Matisse.

8

The fog horn announces the arrival of our boat in Papeete harbor. The coasts are highlighted with yellow ocher and lapis lazuli; the boat masts draw the port in the way of hollowed Chinese shadows. I am at once shy and eager to meet Matisse, whose name has resonated within me for weeks. How will I recognize him? He said he would wait for me at the pier. I am wearing a light silk dress, marked with small size folds. A wide brimmed hat covers my exuberant hair. Mr. Henri passes near me and smiles. When the ship docks, I bring one of my Anthuriums, laid this morning in my cabin while I was having lunch with the captain; I put it on the shoulder of my dress. I wait... Discoveries and reunions punctuated by loud shouts, deep or warbled laughter, the arrival of travelers in Papeete. Mr. Henri carefully scans the crowd that has disembarked, and then he goes towards me and, while holding my hand, he whispers: "Henri Matisse... at your service". I am trapped. Slipping his trembling arm under mine, breathlessly, he adds: "Please don't hold it against me. I dared not reveal myself to you. The island helped me."

The island has captured time and mineralized it: it doesn't flow anymore, it manifests all of a sudden. In the morning, the sun makes my room his. I stretch and wait for the small blows Matisse does at my door: small, short sounds, repeated, discrete, but imperative. I wait while the murmur of expanded seconds stretches. I look at the sea. The time has erased the stiffened reliefs of life and sometimes I get bored.

In the morning, Henri and I go walk on the beaches nearby. I walk nonchalantly. Sometimes for fun, I run into the water and come away wet and my garment pressed against my body. Matisse opens the notebook he always takes along with him and draws my figure in trembled broad strokes. When we return to the hotel, I lean on the window of his room that he calls "My window in Tahiti". It opens on the port. We see in the distance the masts of sailboats, as well as high trees on the sides of the road, leading to the port: a window on an ordinary landscape, but when Matisse talks about it, the window becomes another. Its wooden frame is then filled with a frieze of white flowers with the heart of gold, the trees are just sketched, and their curves are between those of the woman and those that the wind prints on the branches; from classic green, they pass to a faded out green, outlined by dark green. Distant masts are reduced to a single central mast. This particular window intrigues and delights me. Looking down, I whisper my desire to see him paint these Tahitian windows. He clears his throat and bends his long gray beard on my gloved and quivering hand.

The next day, when I go into my room, I discovered part of my window stung with gardenia flowers. The Tahiti window is part of my trip. Another day, it's a big carmine cloud which is painted on top of the glass. The painter reveals his picture to me in a way. Gardenia flower, carmine cloud… What will he show me next? Now, when I go into my hotel room, I open the door cautiously and I lean my head into its crack to discover another aspect of his work.

Matisse blurs the monotonous flow of time by strange gifts: an armful of hibiscus to which he tied small birds, singing and colorful, a Tou sheet painted gold and purple, a bark magnified by an exclamation point, pebbles transformed into shimmering glances with their azure pupils, their multicolored iris and lashes, where their extravagant algae and long pencil lines are cleverly mixed. Matisse painted my body with his gaze, transports, transforms and restores using the island and its stones, the island and its fabulous plants, his soul and his whispers full of sensuality.

My stay in Papeete lasted four weeks, time in which I bathed in colors like absolute blue that Matisse had painted on a board found on the beach, the violent red orchid revisited by the softness of its petals affixed on a mirror, the flames of the Anthurium allied to the pink porcelain rose, whose fruitiness is strange, orange, whose color is stammered due to the pigment diluted with water, the green of the apple or the grenade before their maturity.

The day before I left, Matisse had drawn on the glass of the window in his room, the architecture of the mast of a sailboat that we see in the distance. The drawing, done in black ink, gave the impression of being etched into the glass. My window in Tahiti is constructed by upheavals in time: colors, silhouettes decorations decline according to the mood and desire of the painter. The synthesis of the work inhabits me whole. The return was punctuated by the staging of my cabin: road of Anthurium leading me on the upper deck, leather trunk filled with multicolored glass beads, metal cage full of Gardenia tahitensis. Matisse manifests his presence thus. He will come back to France in two months. On the last night, I found a curtain of organza flower hanging on my cabin window. Would this object be part of my "Window in Tahiti"?

Time and objects transgressed, metamorphosed; all this ended when my foot left the boat. Before my door, a painting stands, wrapped in a soft paper. I take it between my trembling fingers and I enter my living room and tear the rough paper. I am caught by the frozen time of the island. The hotel windows substitute then to the one painted on canvas. I open my eyes on the painted windows: his, mine, rich gardenia flowers, the architecture of the tall ship port, the veiling in which I wrapped my hair in disorder, clouds that the sun colors of saffron, swaying trees. I hear a small knocking against my door. Matisse is there, holding an armful of Anthuriums. I had searched in vain on the framework of the window of the Stuart hotel, revisited and painted.

# At the four corners of month of grape harvest[1]

It was a morning, one of those mornings we meet at the shadow of all Octobers. The wind curled the leaves, undulated them, gathered them, colored them in the entire color range of rust. The peddler of words and dictionaries of all kinds noticed that certain words had strayed into the yard of metonymy and had swung, laughing, their suffixes, roots and other factories of words, which put him into a rage; it breathed with all impunity on the term "russet", whose smoky hearth he then importuned, pressing on that of "melancholy" whose binding with sadness repulsed him; he sat and contemplated the stones on the road which, them, didn't dream at all about transformation. Thus, words were his passion and sometimes, became his rebellion.

A man was leaning on the ground and collected, what do you know, here, escaped words, deliberately lost by the peddler of dictionaries who no longer wanted to subject himself with prefixes, compounds and derivatives. These suffixes, prefixes and derivatives had ran away, had reconstructed in a totally undisciplined manner, in the changing light of autumn. The man took the word "carotty", he then saw before him the mane of a horse with a surprising blend of red shades of fall, and the dress of the red fox, carrying the Latin nickname *Vulpes vulpes*. The

---

[1]    In the French republican calendar: "vendémiaire" = month of grape harvest (September/October), "brumaire" = month of fogs (October/November), frimaire = month of wintry weather (November/December).

man reached for the mane and was surprised to be able to touch and slide his fingers into it. Then he saw the word "equinox", which he took with both hands and examined. He jumped when he found that in place of equinox, it was the word "*equi-dies*[2]" that had replaced it. For how many days? The word was right: in that time of the year, day and night occupied the same space of time. Then he consulted the following words: blush, autumnal, golden mist, "melansorrow", "rainnight". The term "blush", placed in his hand gave him the vision of a red sun stashed on the horizon and trying to color all he could achieve with its primary color; as for "autumnal", he then saw the earth like a huge tomb collecting everything that had left the kingdom of the living during the month of grape harvest, the second month of autumn and the third month of autumn. He shivered so much that he dropped the word "golden mist", that took refuge in the rut of the road to spread to the edge of the forest. The word "melansorrow" sent him to the time of his fifteen years where he fell in the torment of an impossible love; he recognized that "melancholy" and "sorrowful" were the only adjectives that had colored that time of his life. Then, he left. Night came. Clouds had crowded the sky and a light rain began to fall. This said, it was an evening of "rainnight", and he immediately realized that the words had trapped him.

He was striding, fulminating. He wished to find the charmer of words, the one who had introduced him to them. He then saw before him a lanky man with a kind of trunk strapped with bands of vine on his shoulders. He hailed the peddler and told him his misadventure with the rebel words; he wanted to understand. The peddler told him he was a pruner of words and that words were his accomplices. He offered him the word "break-meaning" that was only revealed in autumn.

---

[2]    "*equi*" means "equal" and "*dies*" means "day" in Latin language.

# The "tripping over" devil

That day, the snow was falling in large woolly flakes. The wind had started the game, and what was just a snow storm, all wintery, turned into a stinging blizzard. The man walked, the pompom hat almost folded on the eyes and the collar of the coat pulled on the neck and mouth. He closed his eyes half way, while fighting against the icy wind. "What devilry, this cold!!!" The snow crunched under his boots.

When he saw him, he was so surprised, he stopped short and rubbed his eyes. A man was there, on the side, sitting in the snow. He drew a breath of a long cigarette. Our walker imagined more than he felt, the slightly sweet smell of mild tobacco. He noted the amiable smile of the smoker and bushy eyebrows that partly masked the color of the iris. "Hey, there, my man, is it that you are lost?" The other got up, but his boot stumbled in a tree stump, which destabilized him. Fortunately, our walker caught him and helped him get out of that completely distressing trap. The smoker put his hands on the tails of his overcoats to drive away the snow, and then he reached out "Bilade[3], at your service".

So, Bilade settled in the small city of S. The man who had caught him in a blizzard was the father of two charming boys, one named Pascal, another Christmas. O reader, see point in these choices a tribute to ancient festivals celebrating increase in plant sap and the arrival of the winter darkness. A

---

[3]   The word "devil" in the French language is an anagram of "backfill" as well as "bilade" became the name of the character, but has no meaning in that language.

rather strange chance presided over the naming of two toddlers. Indeed, the future parents abandoned researching the family tree, big name supplier of all kinds, such as Victory, valiant maternal grandmother who had lost a husband in turn gone for a compass and never returned, a young lover who preferred to conjugate love in the masculine and finally, his wedding dress during yet another move, or that Clement who left in the family history traces of memorable anger that had had the good fortune to help him repeatedly meditate on the humidity of the prison of the town of S. The parents, having knowledge of all these quirks, thought good to choose a name far from the family tree. Still, the consultation of the calendar of saints left them skeptical before Magloire or even Casimir. Then, they played scrabble.

Germaine was big of eight good months and expected, from one day to the next, to give birth to the fruit of her noisy love with her merry husband, who in turn devoted himself to her with a chivalrous passion, declined in sweet words and attentions of all kinds, now turned into a lustful wildlife plunging enthusiastically into the throes of lust most shameless. This manner of interpreting love had brought him a reputation of male fiery.

So, they were there, seated facing each other, throwing the dice in turn and attempting to order an overcome alphabet supposed to remedy the anthroponomy of the future child.

"Eh!!! do you realize. I have a surname: Pascal, with six letters!!!"

"… And, you???"

"You won't believe it… Six letters, w and z, they're not honest names with such letters. I found… Christmas!!!"

"Quite true!!! No one will believe it's the scrabble!!!"

Germaine nodded and felt her belly. As big as she was, she really had two in there...

Time sped up and the twins Germaine gave birth to were big, strong men, rowdy, just what was needed to demonstrate their good health; they were mostly great lovers of scrabble. Ah, the sacrosanct surname influences!!!

The slightest mark created an intellectual stimulation for them. There were "You, with Coca, you find what?". In short, "scrambling" games occupied their whole time.

Meanwhile, Bilade son was growing. Yes, it has to be said that Bilade father had fallen in love with a village woman, an old surly maid, a little stingy in terms of femininity. She had seduced Bilade against his will. And from this love, Bilade son had been born. The latter wasn't a bad guy, but he was always the author or the instigator of some malignancy tinted jokes. It was one of these little marmosets that definitely reassured you about your inclination as a confirmed bachelor. In short, people were wary. Few villagers found in this boy the unwavering attachment that we dedicated to the saint childhood whose chubby cherub is the spokesman to.

One day, when he was bored stiff, Bilade son was seized with an evil idea, that of scaring all the beings that were on two legs in the village, including the four-footed. But he didn't know how to go about it. He was only the son of Bilade, whose foot had bogged down in a tree stump on a frosty winter day, and had been delivered by the father of Pascal and Christmas. He had noticed that Bilade father caulked some nights and sang in lamenting ways in a kind of crossbred Latin language. Often after these evening events, there was an increase in thefts in the village of S., such as the purchase of contraband cigarettes, theft of bicycles, wheelbarrows and other wheeled vehicles, as well as resurgence of adulterers.

Bilade son, also called Bilade junior, tried a flirtation with the spirit of evil, but if the seed of malignancy was laid in the pit of his soul, it had trouble taking it. For Bilade junior lacked the keen intelligence that distinguished his father from the rest of the village community.

Bilade son wanted, therefore, to exercise his ability to harm. He took advantage of a windy day to send six

17

balloons in the sky written with letters with the name of the Master of shadows. He was thinking of frightening the population, who would see the word "devil" inscribed by means of these big balloons. But the wind began to part and like a game of scrabble, he mixed the six letters. They also saw a Bilade written in capital letters against the blue, unwashed sky. And everyone laughed uproariously. Christmas and Pascal were aces of scrabble, and they read "excavation" and finally... "Devil".

The two brothers were reading and commenting on Bilade's anagram. The villagers listened and then they began to find This Bilade not very friendly, even unpleasant. From there to passing to devilish, the step risked to be made one of these days. Also Bilade father waited on a dark winter night, took his marmoset which he tucked under his arm, and then went to other lands, more clement for henchmen of the devil and his anagrams.

# The extraordinary story of a very ordinary man

In a morbid curiosity, Jean-Paul Parise never ceased to experiment. And it was the laces without knots with integrated magnet, the "all-in-one" shirt with removable collar and tie, the incorporated massage sweater and AC which had caused him an annoying backache. But he was like this: insatiable, incurable.

This little man, who had nothing distinguishing him from the mass of his fellows, had a secret passion. It was the superb, the divine, the sublime Rebecca, the muse who wore the colors of his club "football" as he liked to say, lengthening the lips on the final diphthong. Rebecca was the appropriate first love, his absolutely green love, as, colored by the wandering imagination born from the glossy magazines. He would have liked to have her all for himself, that she would be there without him even having to ask. But in the country of the *homo* double *sapiens*, wisdom and madness were mixed. And our man was the cruel issue.

Rebecca was for Jean-Paul what the Mona Lisa was for the Louvre. She stood in the middle of his spacious lounge. Made from a photo published in the local newspaper, the painting was framed with a large wood trim covered with gold lacing which seemed to reflect on a smiling face and debonair, but whose eyes had the sufficiency of the woman sure of her charms and the power it could have on the male population without being reciprocated.

She only loved herself, she found herself to be so..., oh... so delicious, that, like the queen she contemplated herself in the mirror of the one who sent her the messages of the forum, dedicated to the local soccer club, pompously called "The club of the brave Footballers of the North", on the model of the club names in use in the land of Molière. They talked, of course, about the roundness of the ball, but what do you know, a roundness called for another, those of which Rebecca was the recipient of, made the essential of these epistolary and numerous exchanges.

Jean-Paul Parise, on the eve of his thirty-six years lived a dream whose shape and color took those of Rebecca. He posted some messages on the club's forum. The content was at once naive and provocative as "You are my goddess" and he signed "a secret admirer, but close", thus hoping that the enamored looks would open the heart and intuition of the beauty. When hormones mixed in and he became mad with desire, he posted more... how to say... lighter, like "You're hellish! I want you!". This particular raw way of approaching things of love made the beautiful Rebecca vibrate. Looking down and slightly fleeing at meetings of "football", she tried to guess which male was the author of this rather nimble prose.

As for Jean-Paul Parise, who, in his frantic hours, assured the club treasurer function, he contented to sigh louder when the beautiful coquette was playing with the right wing of the moment or a particularly well-built goalkeepers.

As I mentioned, this little man with eyes the color of roasted coffee was born in the beautiful city of Quebec under the sign of the improbable. After nine months of a submarine life, moored in the womb, the little frog with eyes as large as the body became a human child. Furious of these incessant and senseless metamorphoses, it aspired only one thing: out of this hell where he relived step by step the change twice sapiens and once homo. He saw the day a September 28, 1972.

September, month of the foolish virgin and the wise virgin had been right of the first decanate of the Libra supposed to rule him. Of the virgin, he had a mediocre size. If the arms were knotted, the spindly legs gave the uncomfortable feeling that our man could collapse, there, in the most heartbreaking way. His meticulousness annoyed more than it amused. However, he loved numbers, in all their forms. This was exactly eight days and 25 minutes since he had crossed Rebecca. He had posted 103 messages on the forum and she had only responded three miserable times asking him who he was, which was exactly what he wanted, and finally to show himself in the great day. Of the foolish virgin, he had a taste for secrecy, the curiosity and especially the brutal and surprising decisions. Badly governed by the Libra, it had the characteristic by a way of indecision that came when the hour of choice was urgent.

These planetary and inescapable arrangements had directed his fate singularly. Tester of the most impassable objects, this passion overflowed the objects of everyday life to go and file even in the computer intricacies. The computer from the club was used as testing laboratory for small programs, like a ruler that was displayed on the status bar with the calculated distance in light years of his street to the star Proxima Centauri or a lover thermometer that tested online the chances that the beloved meets your desires. And so on...

How strange and mischievous destiny is. One day, when the semi-final of the club of "Valiants footballers of the North" against the "Friends of football" was playing, Jean-Paul Parise was assigned to scoring goals via the keyboard of the club's computer, results which were displayed on a table opposite the ground and above the stands of honor.

Fifteen minutes into the game, not a goal had been marked. The treasurer found this to be an unacceptably long time. He leered at Rebecca's side, who was standing on the highest step, encouraging and screaming, and waving a flag with the colors of the club of the brave football players.

He remembered a small program which he had downloaded and had the fabulous function of displaying unknown random messages on the standby screen. He opened it. The machine purred and he clicked on: "Start the series", and the screen went blue. The first letter to appear on the left side of the screen was a "J", followed by a minuscule "e" and then by a "t" apostrophe and a large "M"[4]. He contemplated his loving feeling, put there, by the magic of interposed bits. He sought new posts which dwindled as: "Your equivocal curvatures, I dream at night" and "You are my inaccessible and unmatched woman". We saw there the damaging work of the sign of the virgin who took in turns the face of the naughtiest creature existing in Quebec and that of the sweet virgin for whom the man wrote in baby blue.

He was going crazy chaining message after message. He heard quite a few whistles and kind of a rumor from the stadium, but no goal having been marked yet, he evaluated some encouragements a bit noisy from the fans.

When the door opened in full peal, Jean-Paul Parise held his in hand a reproduction of the painting that showed the beautiful Rebecca, and smiled sweetly, contemplating this new random message: "Little devil, come join me". Rebecca, entering like a fury, stopped stunned. Jean-Paul Parise was the man with the messages!!! She wasn't dreaming. Far from the beautiful athlete that inhabited her dreams, she saw there a little man quite ordinary, whose passion was spread by flashing multicolored letters on the board of the stadium display.

Jean-Paul Parise, caught in the act of the epistolary delirium, wanted to close the software, but could not. By some incongruity of the system, the forum posts had been transferred to the software with random messages and now popped on the panel of the stadium.

The story doesn't say which team won the match, but Rebecca now looked at the little man with the sultry prose in a very strange way. In any case, closer to the naughty virgin than the wise virgin.

---

[4]    Je t'M (Je t'aime) in French language means "I love you ".

# CEO of a day or the story
# of a confusing disambiguation

'As I was telling you Mathilde, Leblanc was our director for two years. Brittle, cold, in short, the horror..."
"You told me that he was handsome!"
'Yes, it's true. Handsome man, but a distasteful character."

Mathilde hung up with a sigh. Her interlocutor occupied the enviable position of general secretary in the equally enviable subsidiary of the Company CONSOMIMPORT, which ministered the consumer with a variety of products which ranged from those "Made in Asia" to those in the French-made hexagonal logo. They had met during these company meetings in vogue in large companies. But during this festive meeting, Mathilde had not had the good fortune to discover the hilarious, the fascinating, the confusing, in short, the famous Leblanc.

This event took place in a restructuring system which Mr. Dupuis son had borne the brunt of. Taught in the old school of old-fashioned principles on the necessity of guiding the valiant worker in no less valiant and daily tasks, he had to retire early.

Mathilde prepared the future office of the steersman of import: vintage, personalized champagne, presented in a box with the arms of the company and a beautiful leather agenda.

During this time, Auguste Lebland was preparing to take his new post. He was a small introverted man, all shyness and discretion. When he arrived in 31 Moulin

Street, and saw flashing the sign of CONSOMIMPORT, his hands became, frankly, sweaty. He clung to his briefcase and sunk as the CAC 40. Mathilde received Mr. Lebland smiling. She had imagined him, how to say... bigger... more attractive... not because he was repulsive, but attired as he was! And those eyeglasses with glasses as the bottom of a bottle! Some thoughts later, they arrived in the bosom of the saint: the director's office.

Auguste Lebland noticed that his name had been misspelled. An excessive "c" misrepresented its originality. When he was asked to spell his name, he always stated: "Lebland, without 'c'". He was surprised to find a box of champagne on the desk with his wrong name. He sat in a deep armchair and with his legs stretched out, he imagined to be a Ford at the head of an industrial empire. He touched the smooth, polished wood of the office, then went to serve coffee, whose aroma filled the room. He particularly savored this moment. When someone knocked at the door, he jumped, caught in the dreamlike delirium and nearly overturned his cup. Mathilde, having placed her head in the crack of the door apologized for the intrusion.

31 Moulin Street was rustling with a particular effervescence. There were "Did you see Leblanc?", "How is he?", "It appears he's one from the old school. It's you're in or out". Some, bolder, more to you and to you with the hierarchy, dared to finally meet the boss. And new rumors ran, jumped, spread. Finally, it appeared that the substitute Mr. Dupuis son didn't mix his ego to the first uppercase person. In short, he was liked.

Auguste killed as much time as possible. He consulted the reports on developments in global markets as well as articles on the "necessary combination of authority and independence for the worker". He found all this grim and boring. However, this tedious day was broken by a number of back-and-forth of the various heads and deputy heads of departments and services that were the soul of CONSOMIMPORT. Between obsequiousness, casually false fluency or near-cronyism, Auguste Lebland discovered a sample that could not be more varied *Homo erectus bureaucraticus*. He waited for the sacrosanct five o'clock that would release him from the throes of the valiant need to work.

Auguste Lebland bore his name as a standard, as a victory over the vicissitudes of life. Mrs. Lebland mother, at the sight of this puny marmoset that had befallen her after nine months of anxious waiting, had speculated that "thin like a thread he was, thin he would remain". To avert this fatal fate, she gave the child a name, bearer of all maternal wishes. Indeed, from the Latin *augustus*, Augustus bears the meaning of one who "has the authority", and also that "commands respect". Magic anthroponomy or unacknowledged desire, it is certain that our man dreamed of being a big Ford or an almighty Rockefeller. And the episode he had just lived in the director's office, confirmed him that something of this destiny clung to his skin.

\*\*\*

The rain dripped along the windows. The noise of the storm covered a synthetic voice of announcements retailed in a monotonous tone. After consulting his watch, Andre Leblanc closed his briefcase with a snap, buttoned his jacket and strode to the records counter. The rumor that had taken him out of his reading swelled. "I have to be in Paris at all costs tomorrow!!!", he thought. The panel showed significant delays for continental flights, as for transatlantic flights, they were all canceled. Leblanc was furious. He was tapping on the edge of the counter. It was already night there and there was no one in the offices. He had wanted to enjoy until the end the Canadian vastness and now he was going to miss his first contact with the parent CONSOMIMPORT, which he was to take the direction of. What bad luck!!! He, who had always shone through an almost sickly punctuality.

He was like this, Andre Leblanc. Volunteer at the limit of stubbornness, sacrificing to Bacchus as well as to Venus, he was also a maniac of ascending curve graphs and a natural elegance combined, with an Apollonian physique, seducing even the most virtuous women. He always insolently managed to sell more and maddened the statistics and the competition.

Leblanc arrived at 31 Moulin Street. He entered the hallway and was surprised that only the receptionist behind the counter was there to greet him. He announced himself: "Leblanc" then added: "Tell the assistant of Dupuis son that I am waiting for her!". The tone was peremptory, the voice brittle. "Mathilde, Mr. Leblanc is here, he's waiting for you". Mathilde hung up and whispered softly: "Come on up!!! He knows where his office is…". Finally, she took the elevator and burst into the hall, half angry, half-annoyed. She looked for Auguste Lebland, but the receptionist pointed her gaze to a great man, with a proud bearing. Mathilde was seized with an abyssal doubt. Andre Leblanc advanced, reached out to Mathilde, then he threw: "Meeting with all the departments at two o'clock. Notify the managers."

Auguste Lebland took his position as head of inventory and when his first day was evoked in the group, many thought that between Leblanc and Lebland, the "d" made all the difference. Some added that Leblanc with a "c", had to do with the shiny side of the character. They were not wrong, because this name from the Frankish means exactly that. And then, the advocates of Lebland with a "d" had inquired: This name derived from the Latin *blandus* had the meaning of "caressing". As for Auguste, he put on his CV: CEO, a day.

# Terra Nova, the poorly loved

Mr. Alfred X was a small wiry man, especially meticulous and highly involved in the professional tasks he had been assigned to. He was part of a manufacturing unit specializing in fastenings, frames for doors and windows, as well as some types of furniture, like chairs, armchairs and rocking chairs of all kinds.

Every month, the various groups making up this work unit commuted between them and were required to achieve new tasks dedicated to the manufacture of an object placed on the market by the company. Thus, Mr. Alfred X took his new position and carefully read the assembly instructions for a broom handle to a screws and bolts system. He then saw his wife using this type of handle which constantly unscrewed; she then interrupted her sweep to tighten the said handle. She never divested herself of her calm. For her, all these little inconveniences were part of her lifestyle, just like the seasons, over which she had no power. Mr. Alfred X went so far as to wonder if there wouldn't be a way to solve this problem. He blushed violently. He knew he was detrimental to all his citizens to ask himself such questions. With the end to remove this type of questions, a little too subversive, he repeated softly, "It is detrimental to question". Detrimental to who and to what? Rephrasing his question thus was almost criminal. He focused again on the user manual of the screws, then resumed his work.

*Terra Nova* was a province that had been annexed several hundred years ago by a neighboring region, whose leaders leered wealth basements, virgin beaches, smooth sand and warm summers. The Cruel War, as the antagonists of both sides called it, was barely mentioned on *Terra Nova*. When it was named, it was just whispered, eyes fleeing and conversations stopping quickly.

What upset the life of Alfred X arrived on a Sunday afternoon while plowing a piece of land available to him by the management of the province of *Terra Nova*. He hummed without specifically thinking of something special. Suddenly, the tiller swerved and Alfred X fell heavily on a clay soil, full of water. On all fours, he examined the machine and it was then that he saw a kind of big rusty box with a section emerging from the earth. He took the object from the ground. The incongruity of the situation very badly put him at ease. He looked around and not seeing anyone, he went home, the box, dripping of earth and water tight under his arm.

The box was of a great size and seemed to open up several drawers. He put strength into it, scratched the rust with a knife and managed to open it. How great was his amazement to discover objects that could only be used exclusively within his company. Hammers of different sizes, files, planes, levels, and so on...; all the material was as good as new. The box had to be pretty tight not to let rust do its work! He hid his finding at the bottom of a wardrobe and quickly erased the traces left on the table. He concentrated on the currency learned and applied on the pediment of the plants and administrations: "Work is precious", "Of forgetting, you should be proud of", "The story is gossip", and the famous "It is detrimental to question". He breathed deeply and felt much calmer.

Like Alfred X, the *Terra Nova* inhabitants enjoyed all kinds of free objects provided by an invisible, but omnipresent administration. The broken or used items were replaced automatically. They didn't repair. Still, all these objects available for Terranovians, as they were called, functioned oddly. The frames were built so that their rickety structure was adapted poorly to the opening of doors and windows and thus, let the rain pass or the cold wind in winter; and each had to go or take refuge near the main source of heat in the house. The brooms unscrewed regularly and for all these tasks, the Terranovians put in an infinite amount of time. As to furniture or where to go rest, their very unbalance put the individuals in such a state of control that this made them unable to think of anything else. As the read currencies required, recited and permeated the subconscious mind of the inhabitants of *Terra Nova*, no one really had the time to philosophize, even in a minor fashion. They survived... a little wobbly and, above all, no one really had time for himself.

The finding of Alfred X upset his life. Indeed, he repaired all the anomalies that he and his wife lived with daily. He discovered that rest was a blameless, unconstrained luxury, although no one spoke of it, as the practice was unknown in the province of *Terra Nova*. And he began thinking...

When Alfred X changed sector again and found himself in the assembly of furniture of all kinds, he read the instructions carefully and found that the numbers shown were the origin of these anomalies that plagued his life and that of his fellow citizens. He also guessed that they had perhaps to do with the Cruel War.

The meticulousness of Alfred X greatly served him. He began to measure, calculate, compare. The tools found became a valuable aid. He had never understood why the children were asked not to run in the house and adults to walk carefully. He had found that a small relaxation from each one caused a vibration of the floors and almanacs, novels and trinkets in a terranovian fashion and landed on the floors. Then, everything had to be put back until next time. He thought that the very nature of the component materials of the soil were to blame for something. But as the houses weren't transferable and weren't exchangeable, he fatalistically accepted this, because "It is detrimental to question".

Still, the tools he had recovered served him to carry out different experiences. One day, when he had mounted the toolbox in one of the rooms of the first floor, he accidentally dropped it and all objects on the boards of the library slipped and joined in chorus tools and toolbox. "Oh, those pesky vibrations", Alfred X growled. The leveling was also dropped and such was Alfred X's amazement to see that the bubble was not centered. Not to think, certainly, but before such a phenomenon, Alfred X realized that even the floors were not straight. He vaguely guessed that it was not directly the vibrations that made the objects fall, but the slope of the soil. This was so much a part of the daily life of the inhabitants of *Terra Nova*, that when someone was late to a meeting, they joked, ironically: "Ah, vibrations, when you can't balance them!".

Alfred X put all his know-how and his taste for a job well done to recalculate the figures provided by his company and to adapt them to the objects which he had to assemble and send. Thus, some Terranovians were able to use the broom whose handles didn't unscrew. They obtained the frame that fit together perfectly and about the seats, they were so comfortable, it allowed them to relax. All this had implications on the behavior of the lucky recipients of the manufacturing from the hands of Alfred X. They discovered the pleasure of having time, just to do nothing and also, for thinking. From the freedom of thinking to that of talking, the step was soon made and each began to ask what had really changed their life.

From a model worker, Alfred X became a subversive worker. Certainly, he put to each object he had assembled and packed the mandatory currency, provided by the administration: "To calculate is subversive", but he brought a small personal touch. The motto became then, "To not calculate is subversive". When the revolution broke out, many of the Terranovians had made their motto: "To not calculate is subversive". They realized that all the objects graciously received by administration representing the winning side of the Cruel War, were built in such a way that their users spent all their time and energy to permanently remedy their faults. And time for themselves, to think, to reconquer their freedom: one. Alfred X also understood that if moonlighting was unimaginable on *Terra Nova*, the imagination of the winning side in power could create it, the black enslavement.

# The loving machine

This is it, I'm in love!!! It just fell on me, like that. A thunderbolt. Yes, it's what we call a thunderbolt. I'll tell you. I don't know now by what to begin, for I'm not the type to just fall in love like that, but there... Everything is confusing. Like what, heart and reason irritate each other, as the great Pascal well said. Mathilde, you know, our secretary that finds all the good deals at the restaurants, well, she introduced me the other day to the new assistant from the Purchasing Department. I have little opportunity to go there where my ignorance is of the new arrivals, specials, departures and so on. So, Mathilde introduced me to the most beautiful girl ever imagined. A gem of a woman... In short, I cracked. Well, yes, it's like I tell you. I wonder if my next leading man in a suit with bow tie also seduced her. I begin. I send her a little invitation via the Internet. Let's see, let's see how I'm going to formulate this...

"Hello, I'm Sylvain, the IT manager. Mathilde gave me the great pleasure of inviting me to that lunch, where we met. I would like to renew the exchanges I found particularly... particularly... - sulfurous –

What's happening? I never type "sulfurous". OK, I was thinking "hot" - well, it was a little chivalrous and inappropriate – anyway, I would never allow myself to write that. For a first meeting, as introduction, this lacked romanticism. Let's resume our text "...I would like to renew the exchanges I found particularly friendly. Could we possibly see each other again?" Alright, I click on "send" and I am left waiting for a response to my email.

God, what's happening with this computer?

Indeed, a cryptic message appears on the screen: "Ddhelp. Error in your program, to continue working, click Ignore…" I'm furious. I hope my message was sent.

Indeed, the message or rather messages, had a good start and even quite arrived. Laura, the new assistant of the Purchasing Department is beside herself. She went to check her email and there, horror, 50 messages were waiting, and all from the same correspondent, a certain "Ddhelp, pretty heart", and as for the content, she didn't even dare think. This makes her shudder with indignation. The first one talks about "sulfurous exchanges", a second one "of a very gallant meeting, and more if…". In short, Laura called Mathilde to tell her about her misadventure.

Mathilde thinks about little Sylvain, handsome guy, but with a very "British" side, which doesn't fit well with this delirium and epistolary... rather lightweight. So, she goes to look for news. You never know, we think we know people, but sometimes they prove very surprising.

Sylvain is in front of the screen, amazed. The machine displays on a blue background: "The system is busy. Permanently. It will serve no more to send offensive personal messages to you know who". Mathilde enters the office. Sylvain explains… the inexplicable.

"OK, your machine is in love and it's blue of anger…"

Sylvain takes his best pen and a sheet: "Laura, I learned you had some trouble with a facetious correspondent. I'm sorry. If you want to change your mind, come have a drink with me tonight. See you soon, Sylvain, R.I.".

"Mathilde, can you take this little message to Laura and put in an application to the service of supplies. For a new computer. Will you explain to them that I have a problem with mine with the hard disk and the messaging software."

# The encounter

Gerald was in front of his screen. He was scrolling through the courses of the stock exchange. It was hot. Elise, his wife, was reading.

While watching the CAC 40 collapse, he told himself that his life, it was a bit like that. Highs: his job as project manager, a "home automation apartment", "in", a stock portfolio that held the road despite the surrounding gloom. His lows, his low actually, was Elise. He had loved her, for sure, but it was some ten years they were on the same road together and she didn't surprise him anymore.

All of a sudden: "Ho, hooo" – "Well, an ICQ message" - It was the in-laws.

Gerald was in front of his screen, but in his office. He connected to the Internet to look for information on CAC 40. A popup opened. He looked at it: 'pretty lonely women looking for..."

"No, I'm actually not going to..."

And this is how he found "lonely_hearts.com". Women, married for the most part, were ready to date the most fanciful to break the monotony that gave rhythm to their lives. The photo of a woman presented with her back with clings "If you want to see more, meet me!!!" Intrigued, Gerald clicked on the JPEG. He arrived to an e-mail address and sent a terse message: "I want more □))".

He went back to the CAC 40, leaving his inbox open. "Oh, oh" – "Ah, a message!" Gerald opened it: "Meet me on ICQ. My number: 922214". He downloaded the software and connected. His screen opened on two windows and the dialogue started.

'Hello, my name is Jean-Daniel (this makes for a serious first name, and then, you never know if someone from the office wasn't navigating the ICQ...)'

'Me, it's Irina. I'm Finnish and I'm in Paris for three weeks – you????'

'Me, I live in Paris. I don't travel. □(( I'm in IT. You?'

'IT as well. I designed a meeting website for people who are single or feel alone. I have a husband who forgot about me...'

'Me, I have a wife who doesn't surprise me anymore, who isn't interested in my job... loll'

'Can we see each other?'

'Ok ;)). When and where?'

'Tonight, ten o'clock in front of the Saint-Michel fountain. I'm blonde. I'll be wearing jeans and a sweater very... very tight □))'

'OK. I'm tall. 1, 80 m, blue eyes and brown hair. I'll be wearing... (what I am going to wear, for God's sake?)'

'You'll be wearing what?'

'A striped shirt and navy pants. What, a classic. But I'll have a sign with my name. It's OK like this?'

'OK, man ;)'

Gerald thought he had been a little too quick, but hey, he'll see. Although his marriage appeared to him as gloomy as the current stock market, it was really the first time he launched in an almost extramarital affair. He had made the jump and with what ease. Some clicks of the mouse and an arranged meeting!!!

When he went to his place, he found a little note from Elise: "Went to an exhibition with a friend. There are things in the fridge.'

He told himself it was perfect. No need to invent a dinner between colleagues or a late meeting. He got dressed: striped shirt and navy pants. He thought of that woman who was also getting dressed, maybe to seduce him. Jeans, tight sweater... Elise with that... no, he had never seen her put on jeans, as to tight sweaters...

He smiled. He had prepared a sign with his name "Jean-Daniel", which he had surrounded with "smileys".

Finally, he left. He felt a little tense. This woman, she perfectly mastered the HTML, the PHP. He had carefully analyzed her website "lonely_hearts.com". She had the air of a pro.

He finally arrived at the meeting. He noticed a woman who had her back turned to him. She seemed to be looking for someone. She had a sign in her hand. She had long hair, blonde, a tight sweater, jeans, hum... very tight. He got close. She turned.

'You, Gerlad! But... you're Jean-Daniel!'

'Elise! you!'

# A software that helps you out

'Hey, Sylvain! What's happening this morning? – You're in a mood!!!'

'Yes, well, I'm tired, a ten pages report to lay and present tomorrow afternoon at four o'clock in Montreal and at ten o'clock in Paris. I would have slept how much??? Stop! The patron saint spirit of the office is there and let's bet she found me the perfect de-stress massage, the drink that boosts... My grumbling disappears as I listen to Mathilde describe me in terms of a rave software who listens to you, understands you, infuses you with the energy to always stay in the dynamic "win / win'.

'Sylvian, it's absoluuuuuutely brilliant. I found a website on the Internet that developed a super-anti-stress program. I tried it, and I can tell you that after, you're ready to take on any jetlag, tax assessment or report of twenty pages. I'm teasing you!!! Let me explain, it's psychology that they put into this software. It's really well done. They're going to ask you all kinds of questions: your connections with your family from your past and your current ones, your life habits, how you perceive the political life in your country, in the world. Then, they make a personalized program for you. You'll only have to follow instructions and ciao stress!!!'

\*\*\*

I'm going to try it. Generally, Mathilde always finds us the best restaurants, the small holding lost in the Perigord that makes you foie gras... with a super offer. Let's search "serenite.Projet1.htm". Well, it's a website with a lot of guts!!! Fantastic range of blue with a music to transform an "Al

Capone" in a lieutenant of the Greeting Army. It's really a program adapted to each one, taking into account what they say:

'Answer the questions as sincerely as possible. Don't skip any questions. Don't cheat with yourself. After you have fulfilled this questionnaire, a personalized program will be proposed to you. Each time you'll feel overwrought, anguished, and you'll feel the need to confide, one of our psychologists will be there to listen to you. Are you ready?'

I am ready. Questions related to childhood, adolescence... Look, what are these types of questions doing here? "Have you had any dangerous enemies at that time?" Of course not. Teenager, for sure, we don't like everyone, but dangerous enemies... Well, they are psychologists, so... Let's move on to "young adult". Ah! They want to know what we think about our society.

Question closed, choose one of the three following answers:

1. Would you say of the society you live in that it's dynamic and constructive?
2. That the civilization that underlines it is going toward a decline?
3. That is has dangerous enemies?

Expand your thoughts in the window below. A minimum of twenty words is required to pass to the next stage.

I have finally filled everything, as sincerely as possible and it's true this program is amazing. Electroacoustic music, voice off that whispers messages of peace or of dynamism, like "You believe in yourself, everything goes well, no dangerous enemy can bother you, etc". I am simply asking myself if one of their psychologists is not a little paranoid on the edges. OK, going over an enemy, but dangerous moreover, it's a tautology. In general, an enemy doesn't really wish you well. Moreover, this personalized program is completely confidential and I committed not to reveal all the details. But can they really verify it???

\*\*\*

*Project Unit 1 to Project Unit 2, what are your results?*

*Globally, each territorial unit on this planet gathers a great number of individuals subscribed to "serenite.Projet1". Its distribution covers 2/3 of North America, 1/3 of Europe, 1/3 of Asia and 1/5 of the rest of this planet. Another six months until passing to Project 2.*

\*\*\*

Six months later…
'Hey, Sylvian, you're looking at me funny!!!... it must be the stress… I'm going to go on "serenite". Oh, yes, did you see their program changed??? Now, it's "fight your dangerous enemies".

Sylvian knows it. The program changed and he noticed his enemies are many. A new test is proposed: "Do you want to discover your potential enemies? Download the photos of the people in your entourage and insert them in the context below. A message will be transmitted and a series of positive messages that will help you in this battle…"

Now, Sylvian knows that Mathilde is part of these dangerous enemies and as for Mathilde, she is ready to destroy Sylvian.

\*\*\*

*Unit Project 2 to Unit Project 1:*

*"Project invasion cancelled. Mission accomplished, the human society is about to implode!!!"*

# Tale of the door of the fourth hour of the day

Pain comes from the joy and pain and woe of the storyteller who believes that punishment is born of pain.

It will make the tale fly to the four winds that will scatter it, but will not sow it.

This story is about the gods of time where they govern the humans and their destiny and each renowned storyteller takes the good fortune, the single possession.

It is my turn to say: this, I have seen it and I can tell it.

To you all, who are listening to me, squatting on the desert sand, know that my words give voice to the story and that is a great advantage to me.

I can, at will, reverse the course of the Nile, overthrow dynasties or drop this story... For this, I tell it... And I observe.

Who in the crowd has a dubious smile: the story explodes in a furious series of fictitious and unrealistic events; a disdainful pout: the story will evaporate, there will be only a few words that will not even be a clue; a gesture of incomprehension, and the story will be told with unknown words: not one of you will know what it is about.

Know that your mission is to give life to the tale and to take it beyond the hills.

If there's no voice to carry the story, give it meaning, you won't be able to give it life.

Thus spoke the storyteller.

*\*\**

Isis-Hathor was the daughter of the Goddess three times humanized.

Indeed, a line of girls had been born her of the high priest dedicated to the worship of the Temple. Isis-Hathor wanted to end the history of this line by linking her destiny to the god Osiris himself, or at least, to the one that would represent her on earth.

More than twenty centuries of a line of men guarding fervently this belief.

Isis-Hathor had desired Osiris to become a brother in her heart and her flesh, and wanted thus to be invincible.

The two lines had separated, and the destiny of men and their riches, not without a merciless war that had begun when the Great Goddess had given birth to a daughter of a priest of the Temple.

The god Osiris wouldn't decapitate his descendants either and, the earth was the scene of several centuries of barbarism where humans served by obligation or by naive designs the adamant gods.

The rule was – for the were rules – that the lines of the God Osiris and those of the Goddess Isis-Hathor should not mate with humans attached to their worship and serve in the Temple.

The taboo of shame was so pregnant that one who would have had some ambitions to marry with a descendant of the other side, hesitated.

Nobody had violated the prohibition, not by fear, but they had simply forgotten. Only Isis-Hathor had fallen in her flesh to the charm of the young god Osiris and it was pride that guided her steps with tenfold martial ardor.

She remembered the dull hatred that lived within her when she went to a banquet given by this master, loyal and much desired tyrant.

Truces enacted by warlords allowed the troops to recuperate well and were accompanied by libations where drunkenness was second only to the resentment masked by the web of usability.

When the benefits of Isis-Hathor, so called by her grandmother, three times worshiped, had taken some volume under her light tunic, she decided that the time of the Great Humiliation had come and she had to make war with the young god Osiris. She wanted him as prisoner, begging, before he came to join her on her bed.

So she armed three hundred youths with bows with two arrows, as she wanted her interposed hand, to knock death by two times her enemies.

The warriors were fascinated by the young woman that the suspicion of divine wrath hadn't even touched. She didn't know fear, only the desire to reign over everything that could exist.

She built a small fort with wood shingles brought on by large barges from beyond the Red Sea. She knew that the siege would be long because the armies of the god Osiris wanted to do battle with the armies of the damsel.

The God Osiris amused himself. He wanted Isis-Hathor. He wanted her supplicating, with a captive look. He wanted her like this and this undetermined siege was for him only a courtship.

In the morning, at sunset, at the time when Isis-Hathor, standing on one of the promontories of the fort, was observing the deployment of armies - which in fact was happy training – the young God turbaned, ostensibly passed before her and smiled.

Sometimes, as a game, he collected a pinch of sand which he blew with parted lips to send to IsisHathor. This gesture augured the beginning of a skirmish that ended at the setting of the sun.

The young woman gathered her archers who were firing twin spiers on the camp a few hundred cubits from the fort. Arrows invariably landed on tents and were greeted by cheers in passing when it came to a valiant archer that targeted the opening rather than the roof.

The cries of war revived the fighting spirit of Isis-Hathor who begged the gods, shouted outrageous insults at the army chiefs and struck with anger the fort of her whip with branches.

At night, when overcome by this endless battle, the young woman slept, her archers were carousing with the opposing soldiers and were developing a game of targets: who sent his twin arrows in a tent was rewarded a few additional provisions, food in Isis-Hathor's camp was under the sign of frugality. During this time, the young God Osiris came to contemplate his sleeping enemy beauty.

He leaned over her, detailing the charming face he saw only tortured by hatred and destruction at the sunrise of the Great Light.

At night, Isis-Hathor showed a serene face, a relaxed body, abandoned under the cover of a thousand grains of sand. The young god passed his hand in her long shiny hair, spread out on the floor, trembling that she wouldn't awake and left, his plan accomplished.

Isis-Hathor, she dreamed of valorous feats of war, of small horns of ivory announcing the surrender of the enemy, the young God on his knees in the desert dust, asking her to spare him and then, her smiles were the softest.

That day, the anger of the young goddess reached its paroxysm. Osiris had passed in front of a fort, elegant in a white linen garment, a turbaned leader. He had stopped there and, instead of sending a pinch of sand to his beautiful enemy, he had blown a sort of a kiss.

Lightning shone from Isis-Hathor's eyes, anger kindled her heart. Standing on the fort, she brandished the sacred whip. This whip that every woman in the line had added a leather woven wire to and carved it, gave power to the one who held it.

Then Isis-Hathor struck once: a panel of the fort broke clear. She turned towards the sky and exhorted all gods and goddesses to a sound revenge against the renegade Osiris, descendant of the god Osiris. She promised them many sacrifices and counted three hourglass measures, watching the sky to see how the divine wrath would manifest itself.

Nothing. The sky remained blue. A light sirocco wind was blowing and Isis-Hathor was furious. The gods had turned a blind eye before this fury and the descendant of the God Osiris smiled, holding back a huge laugh.

To this argument, Satempeftal, whose eye is launching the flame, serpent, keeper of the gate of the fourth hour of the day, woke.

It was dawn, when the desert is cold, and the men wrapped in blankets sleep against the debated camels.

The serpent form was a perfect circle. He had to have heard Isis-Hathor and her curses, the noise of short swords, the held laughter of Osiris. He had thought that such behavior was degrading and thus compromising the future of the gods.

He had decided to act. He stretched the circle so far that his body wrapped around both camps. He made an impassable dam. Flames from his eyes, he made a cross, then shouted in a loud voice: "The bright ones are the ones that carry the loop, the Ankh cross".

This voice penetrated move than a foggy brain, affected by the drinking of the night before.
Isis-Hathor was standing at her observation post and screamed orders. She had thought that such nonsensical words had come out of Osiris's throat and she feared a new battle strategy.

Osiris was worried. He looked on the side of the desert and saw a greyish bulge overhang the sand and surround both sides. He thought that Isis-Hathor had played enough and it was time she declared forfeit. So he strode towards the fort, crossed its limits without a soldier intervening, climbed the ladder, then grabbed Isis-Hathor by the shoulders. He turned her to the deserted horizon and pointed to a cross on the sand.

48

Isis-Hathor finally understood that the gods had answered her call, but that they wanted nothing to do with the battle. She also understood that the road incurred by the arms of the cross were the ones that the men had to take to disperse in the four cardinal points.

Isis-Hathor and Osiris both understood that they were prisoners of the circle and they had to stay there where they had met, there were they had wanted to hate each other, there were they loved each other.

***

Everyone went away. Some towards the hills turned purple by the sun, holding a camel by the bridle, some towards a village of ochre land whose blue and white roofs could be seen, some didn't know where to lead their steps and hesitated in front of the four cardinal points.

The storyteller had remained standing all the time the story lasted. He stretched at length and smiled. He looked at his listeners leaving. Slightly arched, hands behind the back for those who had no mount, they gave a deep impression of reflection.

The young woman who had hidden behind a mound of sand got up and ran to her brother of love. The son of the God Osiris looked at her with desire and amusement. He told himself that men with a complicated destiny as the interlacing of the foliage of immemorial forests were his. He could bend at leisure the frame of their destiny, infiltrate it thus, through the story of his own life.

Isis-Hathor thought that only due to her, the fate of Osiris had curved.

# The dragon of the earth

"The strike rolls his big pearly waves… "

Three little girls with braided black hair on the back chanted this rhyme composed by them on the beach at Kobe.

The sun was warm and they were laughing when a wave came to lick the fingers of their slim feet.

They were walking one behind the other and beat the hands to the rhythm of the rhyme and slapped with the heels on the sand, which impressed them when they came to the word "pearly".

"Maybe we're going to wake the Dragon of the Earth?" and their chant became more incantatory, more rhythmic, stronger. The heel hit the ground too.

They felt the sun, the earth and sang and waited for the Dragon to awaken.

There was a rustling of the sand. They stopped suddenly, waiting for something magical that would have been caused by their singing and the sandy beach became breathing again.

They breathed their chant with even more violence of the voice, the sounds became more acute, the dances more disordered.

Some passerby watched them in surprise.

That's when the sea of a bluish and gray color took on a golden hue and became as dazzling as the sun. It was as liquid gold, as an underground fire that left only its light be seen.

The three girls froze, worried, hands before the eyes, blinded by this solar sea.

This only lasted for a few seconds, then each thing found its normal aspect again, but they weren't in the mood to call the Dragon of the Earth anymore and began to return with small steps towards the city.

At dawn, they had gone to the Buddhist temple to take an offering of glowing flowers to ask the ministering gods to extend their protection to their family.

This ancient temple, lost in the middle of a dense vegetation, had to be climbed a few dozen steps, and although the pavement was soft, they had arrived a little out of breath.

They could see the sea in the distance and the idea had come to them to go to the beach.

They were rosy by the sun and the crisp morning air.

They were running, joyful, descending the steps of the temple. Below, a red kitten was sitting. The wanted to approach it, but its hair bristled and it hissed in anger. They didn't understand.

It was true they had noticed that the birds that morning were suddenly very noisy, then mysteriously silent. They were jumping from branch to branch, or in groups, turned towards the sky, but it was like a flight, a search for a refuge. Their behavior was chaotic like the ants of an anthill that a curious child would have broken with a stick.

They told themselves, while heading to the beach that maybe, by calling the Dragon of the Earth, to offer him some glowing flowers, the cat would become more affable and the birds would resume their bird behavior.

It was also an unusual silence of the vegetation. The rustling of the insects was scarce, the slight breeze didn't disturb even the leaves.

Arriving in the city, as they often did, they paid a visit to Uncle Seita.

He lived with Aunt in a room of six tatamis[5]. Aunt prepared roasted soy beans and tea. The three girls sat on a mat near Uncle. The latter had the eyes covered with a bluish film that gave him the look of a dreamer eternally awakened on his song. He was almost blind.

He nodded several times and asked them if they had made an offering to the Buddha and if the wind was blowing. They looked through the slide door and saw as a vortex of dust, carrying with it twigs and dead insects.

'Uncle Seita, it's like small dust tops.'
Uncle Seita nodded his head again:
'Little ones, go back to your parents!!!'
He turned towards Aunt:

---

[5]    A tatami is a type of mat used as a flooring material in traditional Japanese-style rooms. Traditionally made of rice straw to form the core, with a covering of woven soft rush (igusa) straw, tatami are made in standard sizes, with the length exactly twice the width, an aspect ratio of 2:1. Usually, on the long sides, they have edging (heri) of brocade or plain cloth, although some tatami have no edging.

'Do you remember the great earthquake in Kyoto at the beginning of our marriage? There was this kind of wind that swirls…'

'Uncle Seita, you're frightening the children!!! Drink this tea.'

Uncle sighed and took the hands of the little ones, which he squeezed between his own, all wrinkled and rough as old burlap bags that had stayed too much in the sun.

The little ones nibbled some roasted soybeans, then descend the street that lead towards the sea, not on the harbor side. They found it too noisy, too restless. They preferred a small beach where some passers lingered to watch the incessant waves.

Arriving on the sand, they took off their shoes and laid their tabby beside a large rock with a round back, then they trotted to the edge of the waves and decided to draw the Dragon of the Earth. Each took a stick.

The first one drew the head and in place of the eye she put a round, glistening pebble.

The second one drew the body and, by way of scales, put long brown algae.

The third one drew the tail and placed glowing flowers on the curved top.

Then they made a hesitant round humming and words of the nursery rhyme fell into place.

The Dragon of the Earth woke.

At first, it was a great tremor of the beach. The girls screamed and ran terrified, but the soil, too unstable, made them fall.

Now the sea was rolling large reels of gray water that streaked large disheveled seaweed crashing on the sand.

The sound was that of a furious torrent that covered kilometers of beach. The ground crackled. It was no longer a trembling of the earth, but the violence of the dark forces that had managed to make their way through the earth's strata.

The little girls took refuge behind a rock.

They saw from the city a dust similar to the autumnal fog rise, but this fog was scary. It broke the buildings that collapsed in a deafening roar. The ears plugged with their hands, they looked with open eyes at the metamorphosis of places they wouldn't recognize anymore.

Seeing, but most of all, not hearing.

Not hearing the cries of the people caught in the trap of their concrete nest, those eaten by yawning gaps opened through the streets, the yards and the gardens, those that had become bright torches in the scattered fires of the city or washed away by the giant waves.

"The strike rolls his big pearly waves… "

The Dragon of the Earth woke up. He had had a nightmare. The houses collapsed. Dust had invaded everything. The sea was furious and rolled its violent waves on the edges of the city.

The fire licked the people's houses.

The three little girls from Kobe, nestled near the rock where a gap allowed you to see the window of the den of the Dragon of the Earth, trembled and whispered:

'Dragon of the Earth, go to sleep. We'll protect you from your bad dream that kills people and shakes your liquid sun scales.'

A flash of lightning made the sea solar and a mineral silence settled over Kobe.

Their glowing flowers were bloodstained on the gray sand.

# The tousled child

Plum, small aquatic frog, by a cord blood anchored to the rock of the marine belly, waited that the nine moons should pass.

Plum's mother had disappeared on the day of her birth.

'A tousled child has been born', they had told her. And a child she really did not want, as for a tousled child, it had signed her hit and run.

Plum had become a little child from the old woman who had released her from maternal darkness.

She was a tousled child. The old woman would tell her each day:

'Plum, it's hair time!!!' and Plum understood: 'It is the golden hair.'[6]
Her hair was golden, but the curls were thousands and they tangled in twigs and herbs, for Plum loved to lie among the gorse bushes.

She dreamed there for long hours, the sun touching her eyelashes of silk.

She dreamed of a dwarf named Salse. It was a story read in a book that the old woman kept in a drawer of the buffet.

---

[6]    Word game in French language.

This story was written in thick and thin strokes. Other stories were put there on this notebook with the cover of amber.

Plum took it in her hiding place and took refuge in the gorse bushes. She didn't know the signs written by the old woman.

It sometimes came over the old woman, often scolding, childhood desires and affection, so she called Plum.

'Small child, listen, it's a story I wrote long ago!!!' and Plum hastened.

She knew that that day, the old woman would untangle each lock of hair with the same care she would to unravel a skein of silk.

'Salse, resembling a hairy dwarf,
Slept in the hollow of a tear.

The tear was so long there, resting on
The eyelash that
Salse slept for decades of seconds.

It was a tear of seawater, colored as a rainbow
By the sun.

It was put there, the blondness of a bent lash.

Then, a tremor of the forest of eyelashes,
And the tear and Salse, similar to rolling rocks
Fell together,
In the hollow of a sarsaparilla leaf.'

These bubbles of words, similar to the bursts of the sun struck Plum's ear.

58

She remembered from this rhyme only the name of the hairy dwarf: Salse. The rest, was an evocation of heat, of shaded humidity of blood red.

***

There was an abandoned train station at the exit of the village.

Plum had always asked herself why the trains had abandoned the station. Maybe there was no real station master? Her questions to the old woman had always ended by grumbling or more explicitly, a ban to go in a place where "a disreputable woman" lived.

Plum then decided that since there was no station master and in addition, the station was occupied by a "disreputable", she would be station master and then the trains would come back. To do this, she wore a navy cap and settled near the ballast.

"One, two, three, sun…"

A woman came out of the station and inveighed Plum. What was she doing home? Plum, of amazement, sat on the ground in the middle of a patch of sunlight. She had her arms crossed and glared at this "disreputable" angrily. She was the station master and how could such an intruder afford to deny her access? The intruder drank what Prune thought was "raspberry", what the old woman called the raspberry syrup. The woman sat on the ground, facing Plum. The latter had a hard look and swore not to talk to the "disreputable", who, after having drunk half the bottle of "raspberry" began telling her a tale.

Plum understood that it wasn't a story written in a notebook, but the story of the woman. "Do you know why I live here? Well, I'm going to tell you. You don't seem a child like everyone. Five years ago, I met a man. He was beautiful!!! Oh, yes, as handsome goes, he was, but I was a youngster and he took advantage."

Her eyes were watery. Truth be told, Plum didn't understand much of this story. Moreover, the woman had trouble speaking and that raspberry gave her such a breath!!! It must have been some other raspberry than the one the old woman gave her to drink. But Plum had decided that the station was hers. She was master, right!!! If not, she wouldn't wear this cap. And then, most of all, she had noticed that when the "disreputable" drank a lot of "raspberry", she had tears in her eyes and this fascinated Plum.

She told herself that Salse, born from a tear, couldn't be born but from an adult's tear. He would have been too heavy for a child's tear. And how could she take care of a hairy dwarf when the abandoned station needed her to make the trains come back. She ardently wanted to see Salse appear in a tear. She had truly tried to make the old woman cry, crying herself to soften her. The old woman had gotten upset. Then, Plum started looking for the adult who would give birth to Salse in a tear. The "disreputable" seemed ready. She needed to be encouraged to drink a lot of "raspberry" and there, she would tell her story and this story would become so sad that true tears would fall from her eyes.

Plum would return often to the abandoned station, firstly to see if the trains had decided to come back, and also to pay visit to the "disreputable". The latter drank more and more "raspberry". She walked funny and finally found it was easier to maintain a conversation with Plum seated on the ground. Now, Plum asked for the stories.

'After the very beautiful man, you came to live in my station?'

60

'Oh, no!!! I had a really nice house, but it's because of the child!!!' And her eyes began to shine with water. Plum felt that the story of the child would make the "disreputable" give birth to Salse. She opened her big eyes:

'The child?'

'Oh, she would have your age, it was a little girl. I really didn't want her. Not without her father. It would have been too painful. She would have reminded me constantly…'

"Constantly, constantly", thought Plum, what does this mean, but she didn't want to question too much what she truly couldn't understand. The "disreputable" needed to cry.

'Was she pretty? Did she have golden hair?'

The woman got up stumbling.

'You're without heart, yes. You can't understand.'

Plum ran in the station to look for a bottle of "raspberry" half started and handed it to her with a voluntary look. The woman took the bottle and drank, then she sat with the elbows on her knees and the hands over her eyes.

Plum played an imaginary hopscotch and waited for a sign of the "disreputable".

'I think this child could have been you. It was a child with tousled hair. She would be your age…'

A tear, then two rolled on her the cheeks of the "disreputable". Plum exulted. Salse would finally be born from one of these tears. She was sure!!!

# Letter to X

Through the velvety window, fringed with the fading light of summer, I see from the balcony balustrades against which you were leaning, an evening, when you told me: "I love you, but I'm leaving" and this "I'm leaving" was so enigmatic that I thought I heard "leaving". Something was missing and it was the "I" of you leaving that I remembered by the play of the truncated sentence and misunderstood. It was the eroded word in order not to frighten.

The fading light fringed the velvet opened window that evening, for in anger, I threw all your letters, your telegrams by the opening of the window and the bag was taken, hooked, then unhooked by the curtains of crimson velvet for fall out, with a thud on the flagstones of the courtyard.

And you came back, my infinite. Surprised! The sun watered your hair with silk.

You tell me the "I love you" and the "I'm leaving" belong to another time that doesn't exist anywhere.

Then the sun came into the house, the mirror reflects the world, the balcony is green velvet. And my body is only waiting.

It's been some months since I have been looking for you. We met, do you remember that Monday when the cold was so alive. We clashed. The too violent wind, no doubt.

Our thoughts scattered. In short, you told me: "Sorry" and I answered: "You have golden eyes".

We then stopped. The wind had ran. Time had become silent in the moment of our looks.

By the velvety window, I see you, the elbow placed on balusters of the balcony, smiling sadly. Then you left. You said "my infinite". My tears were my answer.

Already, everything whispers your absence. The mirror has tarnished, the sun doesn't penetrate our door, the foam from the balcony has dried. Since, I'm looking for you and I weave invisible links through all the gold to fix that of your eyes in my heart: the gold of the eyes of the Abyssinian cat and the sun on the lake. I even painted all shades of gold, from the most copper to the most white.

Tell me I am as necessary to you as the sun is to the earth. Tell me a night and a day are only a dust of wind. Then, the mirror will reflect all the trees in the world, the sun will penetrate the whole house, the balcony will be only a velvety green, and you will hold me so hard that I think I'll slip into you.

# To my "turtle-child"

Here you are, at the dawn of an existence that, me, in my most foolish dreams, had imagined, protected by the fairies.

I walked my enormous and bright belly on the African soil, there were the earth is ochre and where the big cats make their long, terrifying growls be heard. A day when your father and I had taken the trail of the "man eater", as the people of the village called the jaguar, we met it, posted in tall grass that the wind made shiver. Our looks crossed, held, oh, for a short moment, just the one to feel we lived in an inaccessible world, both to one and the other. His look evaluated me, evaluated us, like preys. My soul was crossed by admiration and also by fear. It was in that day that you manifested your presence. What a courageous child I have there, I thought. To such a child, the name of a king was needed, a name governed by Jupiter or Mars. Alexander or Joan were chosen for you.

We didn't yet know you were a turtle without carapace.

Do you still want to listen to some stories from the fragrant countries and the time where you weren't yet living in the land of men?

In the village of Ongongoro lived an old woman that saw the child about to come in the belly of the pregnant woman. I went to consult with her. On my swollen dress, she put her hand whose long black skin was as rough as a burlap dried in the sun. She gasped, then whispered: "This child will remain in your shadow", then she fled limping. This small mysterious phrase accompanied me all along the pregnancy without having understood its true meaning.

You were conceived in Namibia, somewhere between mineral stupor and billowing wind. As soon as I discovered your presence in me, I started telling you about all the little things in my life, the beauty of the rock, the color of the dried mud and even conversations in the Otjihero language. There was also an unexpected encounter with a gnu in a bend of the road. Surprised, I jumped and you, echoing, you murmured in your turn.

When the time of the nine months came to an end, I returned to France to welcome you. You were born one evening in June. I was waiting for you so impatiently. We were presented to one another and then I knew something was wrong. Yet, all your little toes were there, as well curled petals...

They took you to clothe you with that little tunic in the colors of Africa in which I had put so much love and so much expectation. Then, when you were put against my chest, asleep from the fatigue of your great journey and your arrival on earth, I was told that you suffered from the Down syndrome. As I showed a total incomprehension with the wording of the verdict, the doctor told me you'd be slower than other children. He explained that when you were conceived, a chromosomal aberration occurred. This means that your world is going to look on the odd mode: 21 pair of chromosomes and the 47 you possess instead of the 46 required. My world is that of even numbers, but we will meet on the way of love.

All this simply means that you will be as slow as a small turtle and you will take more time than other children to do things, but, you know, time is a rare thing that will be yours. You're also a small turtle without its shell and you will have to be surrounded by a lot of love to build a very solid one, as solid as the bronzed gaze and pride of the jaguar.

# The Smugglers

The holographic bells struck in big blows of their illusory bronze hammers of overthrown basins. The gray sky was covered intermittently with large inscriptions, welcoming the New Year and recalling in passing the principles that founded the existence and ownership of any earthling in this year of 2096. The cities had proliferated and the blue planet only offered the oceans as a virgin territory of residence and of the human gender in general. The new technologies, including holography was only one of the most spectacular aspects that had radically changed the urban lifestyle. We no longer talked about villagers or farmers; these notions had purely disappeared from the lexicon, as well as the villages and farmlands or forests of the earth. Urban areas extended over thousands of kilometers.

When "Matter Mater" occupied a market niche of new technology, no one took any notice. We questioned sometimes on why this name crossed with Latin, but the average consumer saw it as a company dedicated to IT and its derivatives. In fact, "Matter Mater" had established an advanced laboratory in which it developed research on the core of the matter. Its leaders saw it as an innovative way of earning money. Indeed, following the highly acclaimed research work which posed as a hypothesis for the transformation of sea water into solid matter through the "molecular converter", the leaders had invited the author and researcher to join their team of engineers to develop this device. The latter gave results quite unexpected; 75 cl of seawater past through the "converter" gave 1 kg of raw matter. But when technology and imagination met, the raw material became a manufactured object, quite like those made by human hands. He just had to create the appropriate matrices and some lines of programs that altered the shape, color and texture. In short, the man had become a god and he greatly praised himself. The news from "Matter Mater" invaded the market, then it was the miniaturized "molecular converters" and everyone could create, easily, various trinkets and small items. This small research structure then became a multinational. And with the improvements helping, it was entire towns that were built in the aegis of "Matter Mater". These megacities were composed of large structures of several hundreds of floors. These floors gathered thousands of people. The craze became such that the urban and rural people rushed to the new cities. Each contender was assigned to such a unit and such a cell, meaning to that floor and that apartment. Each apartment had a "converter", the new users could create new objects or destroy at will, according to their mood and their desire. Fashion seized the phenomenon and new treaties became the hallmarks of a new lifestyle. We lived both in abundance and creativity.

All major cities had been abandoned. They were regarded as curiosities. Nobody lived there anymore. It was time for a vacation, but the social organization had become so coercive that it was impossible to stay long enough to penetrate another way to live. And everyone came back with the regret of something indefinable and then quickly plunged in a fragmented time, hyper-organized. And this is how life went on. To overcome these other regrets, the management board of the group "Matter Mater" become "Magister Supreme", self-proclaimed, had thought it had found a solution by building towers which, through a pioneering process colored with the image of the sky, but in that year, there were already chandeliers whose firmament was of a uniform gray and the regrets were harsher afterwards.

The social fabric had become so rigid that the word "revolution" was the effect of a quaint old song that waved cavils of evil exoticism. Martha lived in Mega12, one of the many megacities that covered the earth like a net with a tight and tear-resistant mesh. She had been assigned to Unit 103, cell 1015. However, some cracks appeared here and there. So it had truly started for Martha the day she had gone into a "curiosity city" at the edge of the sea. She took a courier - as they called the transport devices that you programmed from the start to the desired destination - and had gone for a period of two days. The attraction for these cities was such that the Supreme Magister had erected a Decree, issuing only an annual authorization. Martha went with her two children to this place she dreamed of. When she arrived, she was surprised to see only buildings of eight to ten floors and spacious streets. In the megacities, the towers reached hundreds of floors and the streets were only corridors where couriers quietly sneaked through. As for the apartments, most had only blind windows that reflected in the holographic landscapes that were available at the discretion of their inhabitants, according to their moods. Here, the streets were wide and lined with tall trees and the sidewalks were covered with a regularly cut lawn by robots assigned to this task. All this green surprised Martha, who knew of the color green only the holographic plants that flourished in the offices or the shopping centers and was even more surprised to see that plants growing in the "curiosity city" had much more dense consistency than those that were found in megacities like Mega12. In the latter, all object holographic offered the resistance of a light breeze. Only those created from the "converter" had the density of usual matter. She estimated an old way of life in which the objects, in their full materiality were to reveal that denominated history of "a social unit materialized". In her hometown, only the towers for living were material and the objects were made by molecular converters. The rest was just a holographic mirage where it sufficed for example, to manipulate a console for the desired book.

In the "curiosity city", everything was different. Indeed, arriving here, Martha and her children were frightened by the thousands of insects that had developed there. In the megacities, eradication of all life, outside the human one was seen as the culmination of evolution, Mother Nature was correct and of its strangest manifestations or seemingly ridiculous. A charming magic took Martha and her children. She felt an incongruous desire: to stay here. She knew it was worse than stealing a courier or violating any laws issued by the Supreme Magister, but she was so taken by the beauty of the locations. Something confusing was awaking inside her. She didn't even know how to get to her desired end. But her desire was there, omnipresent, and she closed her eyes, telling herself she would find a solution. She had left the courier at the entrance to the city. The latter was invaded by hundreds of people who, like Martha, were visiting. Houses and buildings were closed and most of the doors had been bricked up. She told herself that by climbing a wall, she might be able to force one of the windows overlooking the courtyards. She wanted to enter a house, and, in an obscure way, she walked, seeking a conducive place for her project. She was especially surprised by that desire that to her knowledge, no one had shown.

Guletry, Martha's son ran and climbed mounds of earth. It was then he saw a bird take flight. He had only seen it through the holographic projections, but there, he felt that this bird was different. He ran to catch it. Martha called him, but he did not care. He wanted this bird. He climbed on a wall. The bird pecked some herbs and looked at the child. It advanced hopping and then waited. It was like an invitation to follow. Gueltry stopped, pretending to lose interest in the bird, so he could jump at the right moment. It was then he lost his balance and fell into the garden of a house. He was dumbfounded, not knowing what to do. He knew it was prohibited from entering homes or gardens and that no one had ever violated this rule. At the same time, he was happy to break this monotonous walk and he told himself that Martha would come for him there. He did not call because he confusedly feared that something terrible might happen. A few minutes later, Martha had joined Gueltry with small Solnia who watched, astonished, this big brother who had brought them into the garden, she and her mother. Martha looked at Gueltry and they both knew they had finally arrived, but they had to be quiet so as not to attract attention.

Martha took the controller of the courier. She knew that the latter could locate her as long as she had it on her. She was undecided. She wanted to separate. To throw it over the wall, it would certainly indicate where she could be localized and then, they would find her. Keep it with her, it was taking the same risk, but she had learned by hearsay that controllers wouldn't work anymore as soon as one entered the houses. But to leave this item would mean she was in one of these houses. Break it? This idea frightened her, for never had anyone taken this risk. Gueltry understood his mother's indecision. He took out a piece of scrap metal that he found on the road and began to disassemble the machine. Indeed, it became inert and Martha knew she had definitely been cut from the megalopolis. She ran, laughing quietly in the garden and picked an armful of flowers which she dressed in Solnia's hair. The latter was surprised and could not understand the sudden gaiety of her mother, for she never saw her laughter. Gueltry had climbed on the windowsill and waved to his mother and sister approaching a finger to the lips, and with the other hand he used to push the flaps of the window. It suddenly gave way and Gueltry fell heavily to the floor. He rose, dusting himself. Martha gave Solnia a push then climbed in turn, and took the child in her arms. The silent, little girl clung against her mother and watched with concern that room where the objects seemed strange and disturbing. Martha closed the window, sat on a sofa, reflecting. This strange adventure seemed to lead her nowhere. She knew she had violated a rule, it was serious and at the same time, she wanted to wait, for it seemed to her that other things could happen. The children had at first taken refuge against their mother, then they began exploring the room and then the house. They opened a door and found themselves in a small hallway that closed a kind of alcove and it was then that Gueltry called Martha.

\*\*\*

Martha rushed and saw, lined up next to each other, tens of controllers. She realized that others had broken the rule. She was hesitant and then decided to see if there was an opportunity to meet those who had ignored the Supreme Magister's instructions. Martha took the children by the hand and thus, they began exploring the house. Gueltry was excited by the discovery of so many new objects and it was a pleasure touching each of them. This was something else from the plethora of objects and holograms he had the luxury of having in Mega12, his city. Martha scolded him gently, so that he calmed down. They arrived before a door that seemed locked. They forced it by pulling above, but nothing helped. Martha began to disassemble the lock and she spent a long time, releasing from time to time, her forehead from a rebel hair, then she arose smiling. The door gave way. It was dark, a staircase was lost in the shadows. Gueltry ran to find one of these dilapidated lamps he lit the fuse to and then, preceded by their mother, the children began to descend. Martha was worried and at the same time, she felt she was living as it had never happened to her. None of these events seemed to be born of an organizing will as she was used to live in Mega12, where everything was structured and where not a space of time was empty.

They saw a large vaulted room and at the end, a wooden door was ajar. They went in there and followed a corridor that seemed to fit the contour of a strange aimless maze. Martha wondered what she would meet at the end of this journey. Suddenly, she stopped. She had heard a noise of steps. A huge concern washed over her. She hurried on. The children followed her trotting, without complaining. They felt this unusual situation, so they did not want to disturb it with anything, be it by their bad mood. Steps went down the stairs. Martha took refuge in a corner behind some crates that had accumulated there and waited. Soon, a group of people appeared and passed her walking on tiptoe, while chatting softly. That's when Solnia, tired probably by this

74

immobility, began to whine. The man who appeared to be the group's leader stopped suddenly and began to scan the darkness, with a tense face and the eyes trying to force the shadows. Martha decided to get out. All froze, half by surprise, because they did not expect to find someone in this retreat, mid by mistrust, because they did not know who was there, although they had poorly imagined that they had been identified by the Supreme Magister's officers. The latter were, more than the others, subject to the pressure that could be exerted on them all by the rules set out on Mega12.

Martha advanced and explained the stupid accident that had made Gueltry fall into the garden, then the curiosity that had guided them till the interior of the house. A woman with amber eyes took her hand and, without saying anything, took her further in this labyrinth. The children trotted behind, silent. After a spiral staircase that seemed endless, they came before a carved wooden door. A man with azure eyes took a controller and maneuvered it so that the door opened. Martha was surprised, because she had never imagined that one could use a controller for other purposes than to travel on couriers. They entered a large room. On protruding stones torches hung, throwing moving shadows on huge slabs. Each took a place on the seats arranged around a sort of circle formed by a series of octagonal slabs. Irvag – such was the name of the one that seemed to be the leader of the group - took the controller again and summoned a holographic circle which was superimposed to the existing one on the floor, then he spoke:

'Friends, we have gathered tonight, in this day of the seventh decade, after our decision to fight against Mega12 and the Supreme Magister. We have, because in the past we called this luck, met this woman and her children and we hope they'll come work with us for the conquest of our freedom.'

All rose and hands on the chest, saluted the speaker.

Martha didn't know what to think. Everything had become so strange suddenly. She felt that what was taking place now was the culmination of a confused and unspoken expectation. She knew she had always been with them, that this had existed before in her, much stronger than Mega12 and the Supreme Magister.

Everyone took a seat and Irvag made appear, on the holographic circle, different colored spots that were the main megacities and each one took the size of the circle. Then, we could see bright spots representing the localization of the different sections of the group of "Smugglers". Thus were called the dissidents born from the very perfect society, born from the power of "Matter Mater".

They explained to Martha that the indefinable nostalgia that every inhabitant of Mega12 felt for a hypothetical and unknown addition, was generated by the Smugglers group. It was a way to give one day, life to rebellion. For, if all aspired to freedom, to tear the veil of time, to know the light of the sun through half-closed eyes, the light breeze on the face or the taste of raspberry on a summer evening, the consumption of all holographic or manufactured by "Matter Mater" would be the worst. And it would be time for the Supreme Magister to be forgotten, forever.

Martha returned to Mega12 after Irvag had taken care to make the controller function again. When she went back, she complained about the failure of the latter. They checked it and laid it down on random failures, as much as they could arrive. There were no sufficient controllers that broke down in the "curiosity cities" so they could make a comparison with the missing ones from Mega12 and elsewhere. And life went on. Martha kept the hope, that one day, she could go back there.

76

She would have loved to see Irvag and his azure eyes again. It wasn't about love as she knew it anymore, but of a more powerful feeling and much larger that seemed to make the connection with the infinity she had inside. She remembered having this feeling after reading one of those forbidden books that were passed under the counter. It was the story of a man who had known, beyond suffering and death, say with deep conviction that he carried the light of the world and she thought there had to be the same azure look as that of Irvag. She felt a light being born in her, but it was an almost fetal light. She felt it alive, like a tiny dot and she felt quite far from Irvag and all those she had encountered.

Often at night, instead of watching the holographic broadcasts, Solnia, Gueltry and her, spoke at length of their adventure. Gueltry said he wanted, when he would become a man, to join those of the "curiosity city" and work with them. Martha was surprised by a maturity she had never suspected in him. Gueltry played, all the time before the others, the role of a small boy from Mega12, enthusiast of holographic games, but when he was alone with his sister and Martha, he spoke again at length of Irvag and his projects. Solnia listened quietly. The years passed on Mega12, without the memory of this adventure fading. Sometimes, one forgot a detail and it was the other two who reminded him. It was their saga. They had learned to be attentive to the world and they were waiting.

Little by little, the social organization, become too coercive, began to unravel. And it began with the disappearance of individuals belonging to Mega12 and other megacities. Then, in numerous phases, several energy failures affected these huge cities and the population, almost idle, who had found facing itself, not knowing what to do. This new situation had not, so far, allowed deeper communication between individuals. Although uncomfortable, people went and came, acted as if nothing had happened, as if this crisis didn't exist. The first two times, the failure had been sufficiently short for nobody to interrogate about its origin. Only individuals like Martha sensed that something was happening and rejoiced inwardly.

***

It was during a much longer failure that Martha saw the Smugglers again. All these successive failures had been at the origin of new ways of communication. Indeed, the development of these surprising and innovative technologies had rendered the population completely dependent on them. They scrapped the impromptu encounters, neglected the crafts, the simple act of gossiping was considered an incongruous social act, almost suspicious. Only those were admitted for holographic programs or the latest gadget that was out. In short, after this series of failures, people began to talk among themselves. At first, the exchanges were quite prosaic, if only to find solutions to overcome the lack of energy: all primary biological service circuits were also out of state. The people were facing facts they had never known, such as the lack of hygiene. The transformation circuit of wastewater was no longer functional, clean water becoming a scarce commodity. Added to this the fact that the outputs of water were in the form of a holographic system, which no longer worked, because of disruptions in energy, a state of emergency was declared and the water was distributed in minimum quantities. Gangs began to take shape, here and there. They resold water at high prices. Martha felt a hope being born in her. She lived like others and was getting used to this new life where their space was reduced to Unit 103.

One day, when Martha was walking in the holographic gardens, she had the surprised to see a stranger. The latter was tall, angular face with clear eyes catching the light and a

78

nonchalant approach, which made you specifically take him for a visitor. She sat near a fountain whose jets fell in a myriad of multicolored lights. The stranger approached her and asked various questions about Unit 103, the one where she lived, its population, she replied while remaining attentive to another message. He reminded her of something and, suddenly, she remembered. She had seen him in "curiosity city". She remained silent for a moment. She dared not remember this memory, but she wanted to know. She was sure he wasn't one of the Supreme Magister agents, but something in her prevented her from expressing herself then. She would have loved to tell him that she had seen him in the tiled room, talk to him of Irvag. Then, she spoke of Unit 103, of the difficult life that each had in every innumerable units of the Mega12. She said how she greatly regretted not having returned to the "curiosity cities". At this word, Geltry, who was playing a new holographic game close to his mother and listened attentively to the conversation, left the game and stood before the stranger:

'I saw you when we went into the room where there was Mega12 in holography.'

The stranger smiled and then, with a faraway look said: 'Me too.'

Martha then knew he had recognized her and it was her whom he had come to look for. She offered him hospitality. He accepted. She met her neighbors living in cell 1014, adjoins hers. They looked at her, astonished. Everyone knew that it was absolutely impossible to join other units. The regulation was strict about it. How had this stranger come here? But as it was difficult to accept the impossible, they then tried to forget what they had seen.

The stranger went in. It was cozy. She lit the mood buttons which gave cell 1015 the color of the setting sun. The stranger smiled, but Martha felt he was not surprised, just the smile of one who had known something for long and who had exceeded it. He sat down, closed his eyes and then he asked Martha and her children to listen. Solnia nibbled a lock of her hair which was a sign with her of a great attention.

The man talked to them thus:

'What is happening now is not the consequence of a power reduction due to a malfunction of the Mega12 plants, but it is the work of our Smugglers. We want to live otherwise, create with our own hands, think, write, draw, everything that is forbidden to us here, we want to achieve this everywhere and make "curiosity cities" our cities. We have long lived in megacities. I, myself was one of the attachés of the Mega12 Magister, but I understood that this social structure was too crazy to be human.'

Martha listened. She found her own doubts, her concerns. She felt that the meeting of the "curiosity city" had led to this moment of her personal history. During decades of days, her children and herself, had consoled themselves with the singular adventure they had lived in the large tiled room. Everyone remembered the events and sometimes, some details were forgotten by one and recalled by the other two. They had lived so many years with this story that was a life-giving source in the middle of everything that was holographic and molecularly converted. Thus was connected the link in the garden full of flowers and insects to such a different holographic garden. Martha waited for the stranger to say something else, but he got up and walked several times through the room. He touched the walls and smiled. He sat down again, and dipping his head in his hands said in a low voice:

'The crises that will appear in the coming weeks will only be the first fruits of the months that will be much more severe. When the time comes, we will come for you.'

Martha found this discourse strange. She looked at the man, questioning, but he got up, opened the door and went out. Martha remained silent. She didn't want to create too much noise around this stranger, because she had noticed the astonishment of her neighbors and from there, they could become the zealous informers of the Supreme Magister.

*** 

From then on, everything started to deteriorate very quickly. First, the ability to access other units of Mega12 had become impossible, except for the Supreme Magister officers. Each unit was living in near autarky and although the problems of survival were increasingly crucial, each adapted to them as well as they could. Barters began to develop between the various members of the units. This started with the habit of exchanging small superfluous objects against those of first necessity, and then, this way of exchange became a lifestyle that bound the group. Gangs proliferated, and some found the way to prosper the trade with other units using various ventilation access. It was taking big risks, but it also allowed the dissemination of information about current events.

Months passed. Certain members of various units disappeared and the questions about how or when were often asked. Martha had heard of groups that had taken residence on the roofs. The latter occupied huge spaces. It was no longer possible to see the gray sky of Mega12, especially as the large structures facing hers masked it. The glazing that worked on the power generator remained closed and opaque. Formerly, it was possible to put a bronzed sea where the waves came and licked the carpet or it was a strange forest that we could show, a forest of reddish monoliths with stretched shapes to an emerald sky with a light wind that raised a gold dust. We could even, passing near the windows, feel its light breath, smell its light breath, perfumed by the smells that you guessed came from a distant elsewhere.

Scarcity became such that, little by little, some residents left the structures of the various megacities to settle by the sea, for even if the water was salty, it was possible for them, through the developed evaporators, to extract consumable water. To leave, the inhabitants went through the gangs installed throughout, and on which the agents of the Supreme Magister had little effect on. It was only when the structures, which Martha called "monoliths for inhabitants of planned areas" began to deteriorate, she envisioned leaving. More and more people left Unit 103. Fires broke out sporadically in the columns of rescue, rubble accumulated there and it was no longer possible to communicate with the levels of the upper and lower floors. The state of dirtiness became indescribable. An opaque dust covered the carpets, the holographic outputs and different everyday objects and it is difficult to guess what life had been like previously. Rodents appeared and dispersed in the different cells, which, for the most part, had been deserted by their inhabitants. One morning, while Martha was discussing with Solnia and Geltry and what they could barter for power food, she saw one of these rodents. They had nothing left but an expensive old carpet she had bought, although decades ago, from a strange man she had met in a "curiosity city". It was, he said to her, a relic of a past totally hidden and taboo. At that time, she had smiled at this speech. Evoking the past, for Martha and her fellow citizens, it was disqualifying because with the current technology, everything was possible.

It was while having these thoughts that the rodent had arisen from the access door overlooking the central square of her unit. She had been scared and thought at that moment that it was time to leave.

*　*　*

Leaving was possible to imagine in theory, but in reality, it was much more problematic. The emergency access was blocked by consecutive rubble from different fires and the degradation of the structures themselves. The only external ways still opened were made opaque by the malfunctioning of the energy distributors. In one of the burned buildings used for the surveillance of the population of Unit 103, Martha and her children found a steel beam. They used it as a battering ram. The opaque wall cracked after several strokes, then it collapsed and an icy wind blew in the room. Martha was surprised. Outside, all structures seemed abandoned. In the space that separated her from the neighboring structures, she saw an indescribable pile of couriers and rubble that reached the height of several floors. She raised her eyes upwards and saw that it would be difficult to reach the roofs. However, these silent couriers, still in an operating state, navigated from one unit to the other, looking for people wishing to join the roofs. Martha thought that up there, she, and her children would be safer than in Unit 103 where virtually, no inhabitants remained.

A device placed up against the opening in the "wall-window". Martha grabbed her two children, one after the other. All three were dazzled by the gray light that fell over them, because they were accustomed to a form of phosphorescent light, which had developed in them a certain ability to adapt to the darkness. When they reached the roof, they called and voices answered them. Martha had to sit down. Her legs gave way under her. She anxiously measured the long way she had come since her adventure in the "curiosity city". Geltry and Solnia had a hard face, the gaze distant; Martha felt that childhood had definitely left them.

Mostly all over, a new life had been organized. The couriers at the control of the gangs came to refuel the whole population. Precarious shelters were built from large canvases made of rot-proof material. It was a new life with a corollary, learning survival in a hostile environment. The relationship between the people had changed, certainly more authentic, but how much more ambiguous with hatred and friendships that were knotted and unraveled over the arrivals of the supplies or of services rendered or not.

Martha was thinking about Irvag and sometimes wondered if she would see him again one day. The children had gradually obscured this episode of their lives, which, however, had long been the subject of long discussions. But that was before. Now, they had to learn to survive.

Martha one day had the curiosity of seeing her face. She consulted at length the mirror and vainly sought there the face she liked to contemplate: green eyes, laughing, a small face suffused with curly hair, full lips, desirable. She could only see the face of another self, haughty, distant gaze, hardened features. Her eyes were greener, similar to a mysterious metal that seemed to see beyond beings and many people fled her eyes.

It was as if the weather had degraded. A fine and persistent rain fell. Gullies carting debris that fell along the monumental structures formed long streaks. A strong wind was blowing and they sometimes had to stay for long days locked up in these opaque homes, but fortunately sealed tight. Martha tried several times to monetize her departure with the children near water points, but with money missing, she was unable to reach negotiations.

One day when she was going to clean the gutters that had been blocked, the rain having ceased for a few days, she saw a courier arise not far from her, but she no longer thought about negotiating her departure. She had her eyes on the ground and cleaned when she felt a hand on her shoulder. She turned and saw an azure look.

\*\*\*

Petrified, Martha murmured "Irvag". He shook his head in a sign of assent, then he took her hand. She closed her eyes and saw several decades of months back in the underground of a strange house... It was far, but this thread seemed tenuous, despite all, to bring her towards all that. Irvag made her get on the courier. She murmured: "The children?" They rose, laughing. They were hidden behind the control panel. Irvag started the device that rose into the air. Martha wept silently. She felt that her eyes would never dry up. Irvag programed their place of destination and leaning towards Martha, he told her that the Smugglers organization was strong enough now to take control of all the earth's megacities.

The "megapolians" as they were called, took back the "curiosity cities". Life was reorganized on very different bases. Many workshops were opened and everyone discovered some talent, some for the manufacturing of music instruments, others for creating mysterious gardens with orchards where unknown plants, but tasty grew. There were rooms where all knowledge preserved in great libraries was provided to all who was curious. There were also women who were moved by the wail of all new babies. Life resumed its course. There were also some inventive minds who fell in love with the heart of matter and imagined a device capable of converting matter molecules into water...

# Transverse Moon

On a long sandy beach, at sunset, the man with the azure eyes walked with long strides. He made this incessant back-and-forth when the glowing waves died on a silver lichen. Each step made this plant with tiny leaves like the creased wings of emerging butterflies squeal. Their reflection gave this beach a metallic, changing color. The star that shone issued at regular intervals long purple rays which gave a particular movement to the luminescence emitted by the mineral or living organisms on this planet. He knew he still had a decade before leaving for the transverse moon. Located at the left of the main star, she looked like a disk seen on its edge. Its brilliance was like a tarnished bronze. It followed the main star in its declination around the planet. They said watching it: "The Big and the Small Source".

Then, the man stopped close to the water. His gaze touched the surface, and in a particular way settled on a place where water swirled like suctioned. His eyes took such a fixity, as the bronze statues of the place where he had lived. He saw that huge place again. Paved with large silver octagons, it was separated from the sea by a row of marble columns. These columns sprang very high into the sky. They were chiseled over the entire surface with a tangle of flowers with the petals wide open, ovoid stars and twisted branches. This drawing was repeated without leaving a place of the stone blank. At the top of each column, a fire that never went out burned. In the center of this "town-square", a huge theater was erected, with terraces climbing around an impenetrable vegetation island. Everyone could sit and see, according to the angle where he was placed, either the tall columns near the sea or forest trees with bluish leaves that stretched to the horizon. On this site, in different places, large bronze statues emerged from the ground. There were griffins, lions with their mouths open and whose basin was that of a young Adonis, eagles whose hair waved on the wings. Their eyes were of a very special glass that gave them an intense fixity. When the purple ray of the star touched them, they took an enigmatic "livingness" and each of the inhabitants of this place could beg for a future plot.

This is what the man with the azure eyes look had done. And he had seen as in a still image projection, a woman with light hair, smooth and very long, looking at him, half suppliant. She had her mouth open like on a silent shout. Then, the image disappeared. Perhaps, was it related with this journey to the transverse moon? Indeed, the statues often gave a brief information on the place where the inhabitants could find the clawed trees whose fruit juice succulent and unctuous, allowed them to live, or the birth in one of these oblong stones of milky whiteness, a woman with long wavy hair and brown that some purple reflections illuminated.

It was the thought of the fifty men that gave birth to a woman. They had to find an oblong stone and the statues were there to show them, but they gave no details as to the place. Then, they had to observe the purple ray the main sun emitted. When it shone on the transverse moon, thereof welled an oblique ray and the location of its fall indicated that of the stone.

In turn, a man was sitting as an observer between the legs of a gryphon and waited. But long before this, they had needed several decades of time to think how to create a woman. They hadn't been previously able to change the undulation and darkness of the hair. They might think about the colors from black onyx to emerald green, but the color of the blue forest couldn't be made. The eyes could only be conceived in this range of colors. Many decades ago, they had all dreamed of a mythical woman. She had long legs, high breasts of a roundness similar to the fruit of the clawed tree. They all had an obscure desire for a being like themselves, but the body would be different, even if in couples. They had questioned at length when they met on the silver octagons. They all felt that this being would give a dimension to their lives it did not have.

A physical dimension was missing from these men. When they touched the fruit of the clawed tree, they felt the volume but when they looked at it, it was a flat image. And between their sight and touch, they lacked the dimension. Certainly, their bodies recorded the touched object, but the view was only an image with two dimensions.

Now, several women had been born from white and oblong stones. They all dreamed her together, but the newborn woman was designated only to the one who could see her at the request of the future among the statues.

While thinking of the woman, a deep silence reigned. The sea itself was silent, not a wave swept by. The blue trees, rustling continuously, were silent in a mineral immobility. Then, one day, the observer sitting between the legs of the griffon designated the promising radius. And then one of the men who had seen the woman in contemplation headed for the white stone, eyes filled with tears and the heart swelled with deep joy. In the place with silver octagons, the missing man would return with the expected woman.

Each of the statues was the place where each of these men lived. Their niche was carved out on the side. Within, a silky fabric covered the cavity. The space had always been designed for two. For these men, it seemed that they were always there to see the look of the statues, searching the clawed tree and waiting for the woman.

Regarding the man with the azure eyes, he was designated to go to the transverse moon, it had been done on a day when the purple beam had become more purple and when the light of the statues had been more alive and enigmatic. The group had met in the square and had waited. A dimensional image appeared. Firstly, the transverse moon and an ovoid hull of an almost gold dark. The man with the azure eyes that had seen the image in dimension was appointed as the bearer of the statuary secret, as to the others, they had long wondered about this new meaning. The man carrying the vision waited a long time until the day when the radius of the sun reflected on the transverse moon pointed to where the white stone was, out there, in the blue forest. He left, knowing he would not find the woman. He saw the egg-shell and realized he would have to penetrate it to go towards the "The Little Source". He came back in the middle of the others and with a look, told them his future, transgressed, and theirs too, since it was linked to his return.

\*\*\*

The man with the azure eyes was thus reliving his past. He would have liked to meet a thoughtful woman, but he knew she had been refused to him because he had violated a taboo, despite himself.

\*\*\*

Indeed, on the waiting day of a woman, when she had materialized at the request of the future made to the statues, he had seen her in the required dimension. The other had also seen her, but he had already made the agreed sign:

90

hands clasped against the chest in silent prayer. The man with the azure eyes felt confused. He wanted to say that he too had seen her, but he knew that it was allowed only to one to see her. At the time, he retired from the game without ever telling the others what had happened to him.

Much time passed, and again, a woman was thought. It was the fifth that was to come. For the first time in his existence, the man with the azure eyes felt a pang in the chest. He didn't know this feeling. Until then, the feelings were like the rustling of the forest. A peaceful joy with some emotional peaks during the expeditions to the clawed tree and also, the waiting in a deeper joy of the woman who might be designated. But this sense of unease, of discomfort, as he now felt, was new to him. It made the world around him look dull.

It was also the first time when he felt outside the community and felt a rejection from them all. This was also new. And a deep anxiety was beginning to arise while waiting for the answer of the statues.

He feared that again, someone other than him has seen the woman and he as well, had seen her at the same time. He asked himself if he would again retire from the game or join the hands in the prayer to the woman.

When the statue answered that day: it was happening on the place of residence of the newly formed couple on a high momentum and the ends of its bronzed wood let fall a cascade of large flowers until the paving. It was by a floral and metal staircase that the host of this home entered. The man with the azure look had the idea to close his eyes, but this was never done and he could not break the consensus.

He saw a brunette, with lighter hair than the others that had already been born, as a flat image. When he clasped his hands to designate himself to the others as promised to the woman, the latter materialized before his eyes. But another man in the group had already made the gesture of prayer in the designated way. The man with the azure look felt a new feeling raising in him, like a brute force, a desire to see the other appointed man disappear from the scene.

Then, decades of time passed until the ray of the transverse moon designated the place of the white stone.

That day, the rustling of the blue trees was stronger. The day before, a clawed tree had also been shown for the expedition of picking fruit.

All left for the picking. They knew the way. They first needed to move away the first gliding trees on the banks of the improvised path, then the path showed itself, as if the first discarded trees had given the direction that would make the others better prepare the way toward the clawed tree.

They all walked quickly to print strength to this advancement to the road already made and then, as the path had already formed without their having to participate, they resumed a normal walking pace, listening to the incessant rustling of the trees, watching large flowers whose petals would open and close like a plant respiration. This march took half a day, sometimes more when the clawed tree was designated at the edge of the horizon.

The clawed tree was huge. Its large and indented leaves at the ends were full of several fruits. A leaf would have three at the most, but this time, the leaves were topped with five, sometimes six. Large, heavy fruits, with a total roundness, except for the stem, which secured it. The colors

92

were ranging from golden sand to the bronze of the transverse moon. It was enough to break off the stalk and then absorb the liquid from the fruit. The men detached the fruit from the leaves and filled bags made of the veil woven of the stone.

These stones that were the material used in the art of weaving by this group were found northeast of the square, at the edge of the forest. They were big brown stones like the pumice. It was enough to take one of the mature filaments, that is to say having a brownish that was a bit metallic. The men made large balls that they stocked at the top of the terraces.

A man was appointed to complete each lunar month the different weaves of objects that the group needed, either large bags that were used to pick the fruit of the clawed trees or long, flexible dresses than men wore at ceremonial requirements of the statues or when sharing fruits. The weaver also created short tunics that the men wore in their daily lives. The women wore nothing. Not a man had thought to clothe them or to brighten the body with jewelry.

The day of this particular picking, the men thought that the accentuated rustling of the forest was at the origin of the abundance of fruit. They had noticed that a more intense rustling often preceded the designation of the place of the tree by the an oblique ray of the sun of "The Small Source" and at the time of the ceremonies named the "creation of the woman", they had to go into their fruit reserve, for the forest remained silent and no clawed tree was shown.

When they returned in the square with silver octagons, everyone sat at the base of the marble columns. The man designated for the weaving proceeded to the distribution of the fruits. The surplus was deposited in a basin near the terraces.

They all stood up when the observer of the transverse moon made a sign to designate the place where the white stone was. Then, the man with the designated woman rose and walked to the forest. As for the man with the azure eyes that had also seen the thought woman, but later, he couldn't say it to the group because the tradition was that one man would have access to this vision. So, the man with the azure look waited for the others to go into their statuary niche and began to follow the man with the designated woman. It was the first time such an event took place.

The man with the azure eyes felt a new feeling well up in him. It was a feeling of strength and violence, of injustice from the forces that didn't seemed just anymore, like the land-based sustainability of the stars and the planet mocked him. He didn't know what would happen at the end of this pursuit. And if the man with the designated woman disappeared? That seemed highly unlikely, a similar event had never happened; or if the born woman came to him rather than the other, though he did not really know how he would respond to this choice.

He walked silently on the spongy earth. He also knew that no one had ever followed another man and that the man with the designated woman would never turn, because he had no such idea.

When they got to the white stone, it was surrounded by a luminous halo. A muffled noise, like a heart, but multiplied, echoed from the stone. It was like a deep chant, the forest rustle adding to it. A deep sense of being invaded the two men. The man with the azure look stood back. He wanted to avoid being seen. The man with the designated woman had clasped his hands at the plexus, in a waiting prayer. He trembled with a deep desire. The chant stopped abruptly and from the luminous halo, a thought woman emerged, which could now be seen.

The man in prayer held out his hands to her and hugged her at length against him. It was then that the man with the azure eyes jumped towards the man with the designated woman. He wanted to make him disappear, but he did not know what to do. Both were face to face, shocked, one by an event that had never taken place, the other by a desire to remove this man, inhabited by a force he knew not how to use.

The man with the designated woman took the opposite path to arrive at dawn on the place where the others would welcome him. He did not want to know of this incongruous event he had just lived. The man with the azure eyes followed him without having an explanation to justify this transgression of rites that had never changed.

The amazement was immense, when in the square, the two men and the dreamed woman emerged.

The one, who was at this time of lunation designated to the weaving and distribution of the fruits of the clawed tree, stated the sanction loudly. The power always went to the one who had been appointed to the role of weaver for that period. Never were the words said with the voice, communication was established from soul to soul. But that day, the weaver said to the man with the azure eyes that it was no longer possible for him to meet a woman born of the white and oblong stones. It was also understood that he was excluded from this group and this planet.

He was now waiting to go into the hull of the gold oval. He also had the feeling that the seen woman, with an unusual hair color and eyes was beyond the transverse moon.

*\*\**

This long walk on the edge of beach in late afternoon had allowed to the man with the azure eyes a return to a time that seemed immutable to him. He felt vaguely that the concept of time that he currently perceived as a permanent present would be experienced differently elsewhere.

It was an afternoon of transverse moon. The man with the azure eyes was standing on the edge of the waves of the sea, his back turned. His bronzed skin glistened in that day without sunshine. He had his head arrogantly held, eyes drawn of a deep blue, a hemmed mouth, he was full of a distant desire. Only his hips were covered with a leather garment stitched in big points. He advanced towards the trees lining the beach. His look was keen to breathtaking worlds, a bright empty nostalgia, tunnels of luminescent speed.

There had been several transversal moons that he was in this village at the edge of the beach. He never spoke.

The villagers were drawn to him and fearful at the same time.

The man with the azure look knew who to heal the swelling made by unknown insects to him, calm the fever with a look. He knew who to probe the hearts and bring peace.

That evening of transverse moon, he brought them together around a fire at a season when the rain fell all day and the stars couldn't be seen. All waited a hole through in the clouds through which the transverse moon would emit its oblique and blue ray.

When the radius covered the village and part of the surrounding trees, these villagers were silent on the image of an ecstasy of the heart. Each tree, each leaf, each shadow was drawn in this blue. These beings looked at the man with the blue eyes and waited. He raised his hands, palms facing the star. His gaze became more one of fire.

Then, he let out a long scream, modulated in an extensive complaint, into a huge desire. They had never heard his voice. They imitated him, hands open, their eyes riveted to his. They waited. They did not know what. Something that could make their lives truer, their smile more beautiful.

There were proud warriors with blond hair and light eyes, slight women with a smooth body and with a fast coy look.

It sometimes happened to the man with no words to join a blonde woman on her bed. He loved with the same pride he was looking at the sky.

Many moons passed...

There was a sneaky storm. At first, it was the dust devils in which dry twigs and unknown insects were engulfed.

Of these eddies, the villagers only saw the first ones. Everyone took refuge in a hut, waiting anxiously for a non-occurrence.

The man with the azure eyes walked with big steps on the beach. The wind and the rain whipped his half naked body. He wept of an intoxication of life. He knew he could not go back beyond the transverse moon. The passage was broken for him, but he was waiting for Them.

They came on a barge of light. They were dressed in long flexible clothing, loose. They were motionless in the crepuscular wind.

The man with long gray hair gave to the man with dead words a bright, oblong object.

The man with dead words took it. He felt it alive in his hand. This parcel of eternity that he would leave this body in which he lived, would become a huge shell of light that would go well beyond the transverse moon.

He wondered if a woman with smooth blond hair and a slight body could lodge deep in this hull with him.

In the immediate, more than the woman with the slight body and the languid embrace, it was the transverse moon, so distant, that it sometimes made bitter the waning moon on the sea or the wet mouth of the woman.

www.ingramcontent.com/pod-product-compliance
Lightning Source LLC
Chambersburg PA
CBHW071121260626
47162CB00006B/2415